JENKINS PLANTATION

By Frances Marshall

ON THE WAY BOOKS & MORE

Copyright©2023 by Frances Marshall

Francesmarshall63@gmail.com

Paperback ISBN: 978-1-990080-45-6
Ebook ISBN: 978-1-990080-44-9

Produced by

ON THE WAY BOOKS & MORE

22 Cool Springs Park
Peace River, AB. CA
T8S 1H3

Onthewaybooks1@gmail.com
https://onthewaybooksandmore.com

CONTENTS

CHAPTER ONE

ENSLAVED

When Dora was a little girl, she lived on a plantation with her parents, Jim and Jane Shell. Jane and Jim told Dora how their family had come from Africa, in 1859, in a cart. They told Dora they were shipped in carts behind bars. The enslavers crammed the coaches with six adults, packages, building supplies, and sacks for the two mules to haul along the highway to the slave auction.

The slave auction was one of the most significant sales of enslaved Africans in the history of Georgia. It happened on March 3rd and 4th in 1859 at the Ten Broeck racecourse. Four hundred thirty-six men, women, children, and infants were on the auction block. Word of the sale spread throughout the South for weeks, drawing potential buyers from North and South Carolina, Virginia, Georgia, Alabama, and Louisiana. The Northern Press reported the event extensively, and the reaction to the sale deepened the nation's growing sectional divide in the years immediately preceding the Civil War.

The influx of visitors quickly appropriated all the hotels in the area and any other lodging spaces and bars. In the days leading up to the auction, no rooms were available. The city was abuzz with talk of the auction. Daily excursions were made from the town to the racecourse to inspect, evaluate, and determine enslaved people before the auction day. People were getting their bids together on each enslaved person early.

The sale's magnitude resulted from an old family estate breakup that included two plantations, Butler Island and the Hampton Plantation near

Darien, Georgia. Most of the enslaved people were from one of those two plantations, so it was the first time they had been put up on the auction block. Most of them had lived their whole lives on one of the two plantations. The auction rules stipulated that the enslaved people would be sold together as "families," but that didn't happen. The breakup of families and the loss of homes became a part of African American heritage, remembered as 'the weeping time.'

Jane told her daughter stories about that time. She told Dora that the enslaved people remained in the carts with bars at the racecourse for more than a week before the sale. They all had chains on their arms and legs like animals, and they had to sleep on the cart floor without any blankets to cover them. They had little to eat, and the only time the master allowed any of them out of the carts was to enable them to go to the bathroom.

Buyers examined the blacks in the carts with little consideration. They treated them like animals; the buyers would pull their mouths open to see their teeth, pinch their limbs to find how muscular they were, and walk them up and down to detect any signs of lameness. They would make them stoop and bend in different ways to ensure no concealed ruptures or wounds; in addition to all this treatment, they were questioned about their qualifications and accomplishments.

The most muscular men and women were bid on first and brought in the highest bids. These men and women went to the best plantations; those left went to the worst plantations.

Just before the sale began Jim, Jane, Dora, and the other enslaved people were moved from the carts and put into the carriage stalls. All family members were put into the same barn stalls. Over two days, the enslaved people were fed nothing but small portions of rice and beans, and sometimes cornbread, to eat to fill their stomachs. They only received enough attention necessary to prevent them from becoming ill and unsellable.

There was an expression of heavy grief on many of the faces. Some of the enslaved people appeared to have resigned themselves to the hand they had been dealt. They had come to terms with their fate as human property, while others sat brooding moodily over their sorrows, their chins resting on their hands, their eyes stared vacantly, rocking to and fro with a restless motion that never stilled.

Jane told her daughter it was a disgraceful affair for all their people. Some enslaved people would call out at their masters, "Look at me, master. I am a prime rice planter; sure won't find a better man than me." If the master were good, the enslaved person would try to get him to buy the whole family.

Dora's dad, Jim, told the excellent master that he was not a bit old yet, and not only could he do more work than ever he was able to do carpenter work as well. Moreover, he wanted to be bought by Master Butler, a good man who would take his family and not split them apart. Jane put her hands across her bosom, made a quick short curtsy, and stood mute, looking appealingly in the benevolent man's face. Jim told the master that he and Jane could have many children that would become hard workers.

"Show the master your arms and teeth," Jim told his wife. "She is a good cook and can do the heavy lifting." Then Jim pointed to three-year-old Dora, who stood with her chubby hand to her mouth, holding on to her mother's waist, and uncertain what to make of the strange scene. Jim told the master, "You must buy us, Master; we are the first-rate bargain."

Another man told the master that his wife had hard hands, just as good as any man, and his child could work hard in the fields and barn. The enslaved man told his wife, "Show the Master your hands."

Slaveholders and absentee plantation owners authorized approximately 436 men, women, and children to be sold over two days. The Butlers of South Carolina and Philadelphia were the new owners of Jim and Jane.

The Butlers owned hundreds of enslaved people who labored over rice and cotton, thus amassing the family's wealth. Mr. Butler was among the wealthiest and most potent enslavers in the United States. The Butler estate was in the perfect area of Savannah, Georgia, and he was a large buyer of the slave trade.

On the first day of the slave sale, there were about 200 buyers present. The rain kept many potential buyers away, and the auction began two hours late. All the dark people were wet. One of the men oversaw feeding the enslaved people and kept them in "good" condition.

Many enslaved men were skilled in shoemaking, cooperage, blacksmithing, carpentry, machinery, and working in the fields. Buyers sought out and paid more for experienced enslaved people. Even though it was against the auction rules, many enslaved people were sold separately from their families. Everywhere you looked, you could see mothers and fathers fighting against their new owners and hollering as they were being dragged away from their families.

The sale tore apart families, separated husbands and wives, parents and children, and created a diaspora of enslaved communities. Historians, sociologists, and economists have long emphasized the detrimental effects of enslavers' power to sell their slaves and, in the process, separate husband from wife, parents from children, and relatives and friends from one another. It was a nightmare for all the families that were sold. The power to break up slave families was a destructive and disruptive force in the antebellum slave society. In the interregional slave trade, hundreds of thousands of enslaved people were moved long distances from their original homes and birthplaces. The slave economy migrated from the eastern seaboard to Louisiana, Texas, Georgia, and Arkansas.

With cash crops of tobacco, cotton, and sugar cane, America's southern states became the economic engine of the burgeoning nation. Jane explained to her young daughter that the white people bought enslaved people to do the work for them. Building a commercial enterprise out of the wilderness required labor, and many white folks bought enslaved people to work the fields around their homes.

Most slave workers were poor, unemployed laborers from Europe who, like others, had traveled to North America with their Masters for a new life. In exchange for work, they received food and shelter. But most masters would beat the enslaved person if they didn't work hard, or do what the master told them to. With an ideal climate and available land, property owners in the southern colonies began establishing plantation farms for crops like rice, tobacco, cotton, and sugarcane. Enterprises required buying enslaved people with all the increased amounts of labor. Wealthy planters needed even more human chattel and turned to the colonies to build homes for their masters and their families.

"Our people, slaves like us," Jane told her daughter, "were open market, and they inspected us like animals. They bought and sold us to the highest bidder providing an increasingly lucrative enterprise. Buying enslaved people for labor had become so entrenched in the southern economy that nothing, not even the belief that "all men were created equal," would dislodge it."

Jane told Dora that the entire family was scared when they were bought at the auction. The master had papers on them now and told them to walk down the river road, or he would beat them. The masters all had whips and would hit anyone on the back who didn't listen to them. It didn't take long for them to get moving.

The treatment of enslaved people in the United States varied by time and place but was generally brutal. Whipping and rape were routine for all women, but not in front of white outsiders or even the plantation owner's family. The masters or their people would take the slave women back to the forest where no one could hear the screams inside the house. An enslaved person was sometimes required to whip other enslaved people. They forced family members and other enslaved people to watch. None of the runaways returned voluntarily to slavery or even stated they were sorry they had fled because they had been better off enslaved.

"I do not believe there ever was a slave who did not long for liberty. We all whispered at night about going to the promise-land and being free. I know that slave-owners took plenty of pains to make the free states believe that the enslaved people were happy, but that was not always true," Jane told Dora. "The darkies were careful not to show any uneasiness when white men asked them about freedom. Every enslaved person knew that if they showed any discontent, they would be treated worse and worked harder for it. So, when we were alone, all our talks were about liberty and freedom!" Jane told Dora, "Since the government allowed harsh treatment to enslaved people, they suffered physical abuse. After the sale of cash crops, tobacco, cotton, and sugar cane, America's southern states became the economic engine of the burgeoning nation." Jane explained to her young daughter that the white people bought enslaved people to work the fields around their homes.

On large plantations, the person who directed the daily work of the enslaved people was the overseer, usually a white man but occasionally an enslaved black man- a 'driver' promoted to the position by his master. Some plantations had a white overseer and a black driver. Building a commercial enterprise out of the wilderness required labor, and many white folks bought enslaved people where the master was often absent. Of white overseers, formerly enslaved people related harsh memories. Black drivers' memories were more varied; this reflected the ambiguous state between power and impotence that the black slave driver inhabited.

A few years after the sale, Dora, and her family, were traded to Joe Jenkins. When Master Joe bought them, Jim was put in the fields working and picking cotton. On weekends he built houses for the white master's families. One morning Jim's master, Joe Jenkins, told him he wanted Jim and three other enslaved people to make a three-story home for him. Jim knew how to work in a sawmill, and the following day started working on cutting logs for the home. Jim's helpers carried the boards and placed them in a pile where they built the house. Jim knew his master wanted the home made quickly and well, and he didn't waste time. He worked sixteen hours a day. Joe was an excellent Master to all his slaves, but when he wanted something done, he wanted it done now.

Jane and Dora carried food and laid a board on the ground to set the food on. Jim stood up, telling the others what to do while he ate, then allowed the other men to take turns eating. They had the foundation done by nightfall and the first-floor boards cut and ready to work on the floors the next day.

Jim was tired and dirty at the end of the day, but he put up all the tools in the shed and headed for the small one-room cabin the master let him build for his family. They only had small mattresses in each corner, but it was better than the hay in the barn. Jim hauled water from the river to wash the dirt off his body before lying beside his sweet wife, Jane. Dora was fast asleep in the other corner. Before going to sleep, Jim and Jane talked in a low voice about their freedom.

The following day the foundation was dry and ready for Jim and his helpers to put the first floor down. Jim told one of the men to bring the nails and hammers out of the shed to get started. They still had to cut the boards for the second floor that day. The master wanted the house finished and ready to move into in a week. It was five in the morning and already getting hot. Jim brought a jug of water, so he didn't have to return to the cabin to get water out of the bucket. By one o'clock, the floor was being laid, and everyone was cutting and carrying the boards over to the second floor. As Jim was still cutting up logs, he told the other two men to go ahead and start working on the second floor.

One of the men hit his finger with a hammer and caused it to bleed. The quality of medical care for enslaved people is uncertain. However, years later, some historians said that because slaveholders wished to preserve the value of their slaves, they provided quality care. Jim talked to Master Joe about the injury and got some medicine and a bandage. The man could still work with the other hand and continued to help Jim with the work.

Most plantation owners and doctors balanced a plantation's need to coerce as much labor as possible from the enslaved person without causing death, infertility, or reduced productivity. The effort by planters and doctors to provide sufficient living resources enabled their slaves to remain productive and bear many children. The impact of diseases and injuries on populations in the slave society reflected their different environmental exposures and living circumstances.

By the fourth day, Jim and his workers had the walls up and worked on the roof. By the end of the week, all that was left to do was the inside work. There was a reception room, parlor, dining room, living room with library, main bedroom and Pam's bath, kitchen, pantry, breezeway, and a porch to go out on the first floor. There was a chamber with closets and a bath, three more chambers with just cabinets, and a balcony on the second floor. The next floor was the attic. All the slave quarters were in the basement. There were windows in the front living room facing the front porch. The porch had oversized rocking chairs for the master and his mistress to sit in the mornings.

Mistress Pam and Master Joe provided directions on decorating the house. The stairway had beautiful grey steps, with crystal chandeliers on both sides. A beautiful rug was at the bottom of the stairs in the breezeway by the front door. An oversized desk was in the parlor, with three beautiful chairs in front of the desk and one behind. Three more chairs were around the room, there were books on the walls, and a beautiful warm fireplace in the corner. To the right was a sitting room with nice chairs around a lovely coffee table for the men to sit and talk. The living room had Queen Anne furniture with a yellow rug with a star in the middle. Pam picked out wicker furniture for the sitting room to sit in while she knitted in the evening. Another room was long with china cabinets along the wall. The dining room had a long table and chairs to seat sixteen people, and a buffet. The back walkway was a cobblestone brick wall with bushes and flowers for the morning coffee area.

Dora was five and was helping her mama in Master Joe's kitchen. Jane told Dora to pull a chair up to the table, so she could show her how to peel potatoes. Dora was so excited that she ran and pulled at the chair with her mama's help.

Jane reached over, took the potato, and told Dora, "Let me show you how not to peel a lot of the potatoes away."

It took Dora a while, but she did a good job. Dora cut the potatoes in half; Jane washed them and put them on the stove. Next was the meat. Jane walked over and showed Dora how to tenderize the meat and put it in the oven. Dora was so excited. Her mama told her she was doing a great job. Next, Jane went to the table to make a pie and let Dora roll out the crust. Dora had flour all over her but rolled the dough out until smooth. Dora and Jane cut up all the apples, put them in the pie, and then into the oven. They set the timer to cook for forty-five minutes. Jane and Dora had the meat on, the potatoes cooking, and the pie in the oven. They had already made the beans; the only thing left was the homemade cornbread.

Jane told Dora, "Let's sit down for five minutes, and if someone comes in the kitchen, act like you are working."

Master Jenkins allowed Jane to run the kitchen. Before being traded to Master Jenkins, Jane had run the kitchen at the Butler plantation.

Jane told Dora, "We need to set the dining room table for Master Jenkins and Mistress Pam." Jane told Dora to help her get the plates and silverware out with white napkins and bring them to the dining room. First, Jane showed Dora how to spread the tablecloth out over the long table and put the plates, napkins, and dinnerware in the right place.

Jane and Dora finished setting the table and went out to the flower garden to tell the gardener to pick a large bouquet for the table. Jane and Dora brought the flowers in and arranged them in a large vase that wasn't too tall afor the table. The Master and Mistress liked to be able to talk over the flowers.

At noon on the dot, the Master and Mistress sat at the table and rang a bell to let Jane know they were ready for dinner. Jane and Dora brought in all the food and served them. They did not speak unless spoken to.

The Master had the congressman from Georgia and his wife seated at the table. Master Joe Jenkins talked to the congressman about the government wanting a civil war to free the enslaved people. The congressman from Georgia told Master Jenkins (with the enslaved people standing in the dining room) that something big was looming.

"I know you've felt it in the pit of your stomach. I know that you think the market is going up for all the wrong reasons and will soon come crashing down between the North and South about the enslaved people. I can't tell you when things have gotten this bad, Jenkins; America has gone wrong. People continue to vote for the most corrupt government in U.S. history, but I hope Lincoln will be better than the last president. People from both sides are unhappy about it, and I can tell that people are starting to notice. Maryland, California, Colorado, and Texas all have secession movements underway. Congress is so divided. It allowed the government to shut down. Some are saying it looks like a Civil War is getting closer. I have created a highly controversial report outlining some of the main reasons this country has gone downhill and what concerned citizens like you are doing about it." The congressman said, "Jenkin's it's called: "America: On the Brink of Civil War?" It's a must-read for anyone afraid of disappearing rights and liberties or those who are simply wondering what is going on in America. I want to give it to you, Joe."

"This Civil War will be fought between northern states loyal to the Union and southern states that have seceded from the Union to form the Confederate States of America." The congressman told Joe as they ate. "If there is a Civil War, it will result from the long-standing controversy over the enslavement of blacks."

Joe agreed with the congressman; as Jane poured them more coffee, it sounded like it would be an all-out fight.

The Civil War in the United States began in 1861, after decades of simmering tensions between northern and southern states over slavery rights and westward expansion. The election of Abraham Lincoln in 1860 caused seven southern states to secede and form the Confederate States of America. Four more states soon joined them.

Master Jenkins needed to buy another fieldhand to pick cotton. He had already been to the slave exchange broker and could not find any. He knew he would have to buy the slaves from the slave traders. Master Jenkins hated to deal with the slave traders as they were always mean to their slaves.

Upon going to town, he saw a line of enslaved people by the boats that had just come in. He counted ten, bound together by iron collars and chains on their legs. The enslaved people were having difficulty walking to the corner where he was waiting. They kept their eyes down, looking at the hot dirty road. The owner told the enslaved people to get into the shade of the trees. They fell to the grass together with their arms thrust out in front of them to break their fall. The slave trader had his whip by his side. But didn't use it.

"All it takes is money. They are all for sale," he said as he pointed toward the enslaved people.

"How much for the fieldhand?" Master Jenkins asked.

"Seven hundred," the man said.

Master Jenkins told him he would give him eight hundred for two, and the trader agreed to let him have an enslaved man and his wife. A slave girl was in the corner watching them. Master Jenkins asked him how much for the slave girl and was told three hundred. Master Jenkins countered and said he would give him a thousand for all three.

The trader reached down, undid the chains, and told Jenkins to take them. "The girl is a good field hand. She is eleven and will work well for you."

Watching them from the corner, the slave girl looked in their direction. Then, knowing they must be talking about her, she straightened her legs and propped herself against a tree. She looked up at Master Jenkins when he came over. He held out his hand and helped her up.

The enslaved people were wearing rags, so Master Jenkins went across the street and bought them work clothes. He handed the man a thousand dollars and helped the girl into the wagon. The slave trader gave Master Jenkins a bill of sale for all three enslaved people. Master Jenkins asked the girl's name, but the slave trader didn't know. Joe called her Joan.

Joan was tiny. Her head came up to the master's chest. Joe realized she was probably too small to be a field hand but thought she would be a perfect maid for his bride-to-be. Thinking of Pam, he wished he could go and visit her but didn't know what to do with the enslaved people. He and Pam were to be married in just a few months. The house that Jim was building for him was to be a wedding present to Mistress Pam.

Master Jenkins studied the girl as they waited to get on the ferry boat. She needed a bath badly; her hair was tangled with mud. She watched the ferry as the boatman directed them to board and pull over to the right with the horses and wagon. Joe let all the enslaved people down and walked on the deck to the bathroom. He kept his eyes on them, thinking they might try to escape.

The ferry had many animals in crates transporting them across the river. Joan, the girl, watched them as she stood by the railing. When they reached the other side, Jim motioned for Joan to get the horse tied to the rail and bring it to him. Joan did what she was supposed to. When Joan got to him, he got on his horse and gave her his hand so he could pull her up behind him; he gave the horse a slight bump in the side, and away they went. One of the men he had brought with him drove the wagon. It was getting late and hard to see, but Joe knew the road well. When he finally returned to the plantation, he got Jane to set a cot up on the front porch for the girl to sleep. Then, he took the man and woman to a shed with hay for their bed for the night. On the way out, he locked the shed so they couldn't escape.

FURNITURE BUYING

Jim and his helpers finished the home by the end of the week. After having his foreman put the new workers in the cotton field, Joe rode to town in the wagon to get Pam to help him pick out the remaining furniture. Pam's parents had a home in town on Court Street. Arriving at the home he knocked on the door. Pam's parents' butler opened the door and showed Master Jenkins into the foyer. Pam came down the stairs and saw her husband-to-be standing by the door and was excited to see him. She ran down the stairs and hugged and kissed him.

Joe told her he had come to get her to buy furniture to her liking. Pam had a buggy and suggested they take it. Joe opened the front door for her and took her arm to walk down the steps from the front porch. Pam's slave, who worked in the barn, brought the buggy with two horses around to the front and helped her into the seat. Joe climbed up into the cart and took the reins from the enslaved person.

Joe and Pam pulled up to one of the two furniture stores in town. Joe got down and helped Pam down the step to go inside. Pam was excited to get inside the store. The owner met them at the door and was ready to help them. Nothing stirred emotions in Pam quite like decorating her new antebellum home. Most of the house had already been trimmed, but the upstairs bedrooms still needed furniture. Pam wanted a beautiful bedroom for herself and one for them both. When they finally finished picking out the table for all five bedrooms and the two baths upstairs, they asked the owner to have the furniture delivered and set up the next day.

Joe laughed as he helped Pam out the door and into the buggy. He told her, "I am taking you to the nicest cafe in town for dinner." They walked in and were seated in a cozy corner where they ordered a steak dinner for two.

Joe told Pam about the slave girl, Joan, and how he wanted to have one of his plantation kitchen's slaves, Jane, train her to be Pam's maid. Joe told her Jane worked in the kitchen with her daughter, Dora, who was now old enough to work in the kitchen and cotton field.

Dora and Joan were born into slavery so neither was ever taught to read or to write. Dora didn't want to be like the other slaves and be illiterate. So, she went to Master Jenkins and asked If he had any children's books for her to use. Joe told her to come to the parlor, where he handed her two books. Dora worked hard to learn. Never having anyone to read to her didn't make it an easy task. However, she wanted to know, be free, and be a schoolteacher. So, every night, after she had worked all day, she sounded out more words learning how to pronounce them correctly.

Joan was from another country, never having been educated, she was illiterate, couldn't speak English or even tell time. Since Dora had become so good at English, her mother told her to teach Joan. Dora set up a desk beside hers for them to study together. After spending a couple of hours together, Dora was unsuccessful. She was unable to teach Joan even a few words.

Feeling dejected, Dora went to her room and lay on her bed. This task seemed impossible! Dora tried to figure out a way she could teach Joan. Moments later, Joan burst into her room. She tried to say Dora's name, but " Dore " was all that was coming out. Dora didn't care that she couldn't pronounce her name perfectly. She jumped up, hugged her, and danced around the room. She was so excited Joan could say her name. Even though it was just one word, it was a start. Dora's mind started going wild, planning what to teach Joan next.

The next day Dora had five new words she hoped to teach Joan how to say and maybe even spell. Dora led her down to the back of the cabin, where she had their desks set up. Dora worked with Joan for an hour, teaching her a few more words.

In the year before the outbreak of the Civil War, Master Jenkins owned eighteen enslaved people. He spent a considerable amount of money on his plantation over the years. As the plantation economy grew, so did the need for skilled slave labor. Good carpenters were paid the most money. Typically, such skilled laborers provided good use on the plantation. In many cases, they offered an additional source of income for the owners, who sold the products made by the enslaved people.

Master Jenkins was hoping to have many pieces of cotton this year. He had enslaved men, women, and children working in his fields. Although American enslavers bought most enslaved people for fieldwork, enslaved people could be found everywhere on the plantation.

Joe brought Pam to the plantation and showed Pam the slave girl, Joan. Pam didn't pay much attention to the girl whe was too excited to see her new home now that it was all decorated. Pam was dressed in a beautiful long dress and carried a bouquet Joe had bought her. Joe took her by the arm and showed her every room. She was like a little kid going from room to room, so excited to see it all.

Pam planned to have her wedding and party dress made by Miss Betty Shoppe in town. She showed Miss Betty a design she wanted for her dress, but the fabric had to be ordered from New York. Pam told Miss Betty that she wanted only the finest. She wanted aqua silk with a dropped neckline and leg-of-mutton sleeves. She told Miss Betty to tuck rosettes of pink silk into every fold of the full skirt. Pam told her she would come in for a fitting when the fabric arrived. Pam's father was paying for everything and wanted his daughter's prettiest party and wedding dress.

Pam couldn't wait to ride to Miss Betty Shoppe to see the fabric when it came in. When Pam entered the shop, Miss Betty told her that she believed this would be the prettiest dress she had ever made. Miss Betty told her she would work day and night to finish it in time for the party. Pam wanted to stay longer and discuss her wedding dress but explained she wasn't feeling well; it was sweltering in the shop.

When she arrived at Joe's plantation, he told her the heat was expected, even though it was still early in the morning. "It'll be hotter than this out there on the cotton fields for the slaves," Joe said as he went out to bring the enslaved people in the field some water. There wasn't much breeze, and he didn't want them getting heatstroke.

When Pam entered the parlor, Jane saw her and told her she looked pale. Pam told her that she thought that it was just nerves. Jane agreed, saying it was perfectly normal with the wedding; she told Pam to sit while she went to get her a cold drink. A few minutes later, Joan slowly walked into the parlor carrying a tray with water goblets. Even though Joan knew how to take trays, Jane hovered right behind her, just in case.

Pam looked at Joan like it was the first time she had ever laid eyes on the girl. She asked Jane if Joan could learn to be a housemaid. Jane told her that Joan had a ways to go, but she was teaching her, and Joan was catching on fast. She said Dora was teaching her how to read and write English. When Pam asked her how old Joan was, she was told Joan was eleven.

"You see, she learns what she needs to learn," Pam said. She was glad she was going to have someone to help her. "I want to see her fully trained before she becomes my maid."

The party and the wedding were to be at the Jenkins' plantation. Jane ordered everyone to clean the new home two days before the party. Joan shadowed Jane as she moved through the house like a general telling everyone what to do. She ordered the other servants in a tone that invited no backtalk. Jane wanted everything to look suitable for Joe and Pam's families and friends. She had Dora and Joan shining and cleaning every inch of the new home; she walked behind them to ensure they didn't miss anything.

The guest bedrooms were cleaned for the night in preparation for the guests that came a long way and needed to stay. Joan and Dora cut fresh flowers and put them in vases with a water bowl, a pitcher, and fresh white towels on the dresser so guests could freshen up. The chandeliers were sparkling going down the stairway.

It was Jane's job to set up a committee to attend to each of the duties for the Victorian dance. She had one committee send out invitations for the dance. The invitations stated that the Victorian party would end at midnight. Two committees were chosen as ballroom dancing floor managers at the ball to see that the seats were full and dancing partners were available. They also directed the music and answered any questions.

The refreshments committee was to provide for the guests during the evening. A refreshment room was necessary for anyone that wanted to stand and talk. Jane had a committee that would serve the guests in the refreshment room. Tea, coffee, liquids, biscuits, cakes, cracker bonbons, cold tongues, and sandwiches were on trays. The enslaved men wore tuxes and carried trays of drinks around the room to guests.

There was a separate room where the supper would take place. Jane and the kitchen slaves worked non-stop preparing the food. Jane made sure fowl, ham, tongue, deer, and other delicacies were available. There were biscuits, butter, jellies, trifle, and tipsy cake at the dinner. The wine was added at discretion. Jane and the kitchen enslaved people prepared and carved the food they had to serve. Jane made sure the fowls were cut up and held together by ribbons. She ensured that ice was available for any foods that required it.

The morning of the party Pam was lying in bed thinking about the party. She had spent the night at the plantation in the bedroom that was to belong to her. She knew she needed to get up but wanted to stay there for a few more minutes. Joan, Pam's maid, knocked on Pam's door and entered with a tray of orange juice, toast, and eggs. Joan set the tray aside and put Pam's bed tray across her lap. Pam was so hungry she couldn't wait to taste her coffee. Joan poured Pam's coffee and handed the cup to her. Pam loved coffee, and Jane always did a great job making coffee every morning.

Pam told Joan to prepare her bath and to lay out her party dress for later that night. Joan was doing a great job and ensured everything was done just like Pam wanted. Pam had Joan put her best soap in the water so she would smell wonderful for Joe when he returned from the fields. After Pam was dressed and had finished her hair, Joe walked in. He held her around the waist and kissed her on the neck. Joan discretely took Pam's tray and left the room. Joe kissed Pam for a long time; she laughed at him and told him he had to wait until later; she had a lot to do before the party.

That evening, before the party started, Pam had Joan and Dora help her get into her beautiful dress. First, they tightened Pam's corsets so tightly that prolonged wearing could alter her shape. It was painful, but Pam wanted to look her best for her husband-to-be. Next was the silk slip. Dora and Joan helped her get it over her head. Finally, Pam finished her hair by putting it on a back roll. She had small feathers that were the style for her hair that she added last. Pam picked up a lovely bracelet that was perfect for those who dance, and she loved to dance. Pam was glad she was young and slender and had blonde hair.

Before Pam left her room to go downstairs, she put on her matching shoes. As she came to the top of the stairs, she put on her white silk gloves and slowly started the walk down. Once Pam reached the bottom of the stairs Joe would take her arm and escort her into the ballroom.

Joe's attire was strictly defined. He was wearing a black superfine dress coat, a pair of well-fitting pants of the same color, and an aqua-colored silk vest to match Pam's dress. The suit was the absolute best cloth and the latest style for the cut. His waistcoat was low to disclose an ample shirtfront, fine, and delicately plaited; his shirt was not embroidered but had small gold studs for decoration. He had a black tie, but not silk. Joe had set everything off with a pair of patent leather boots with low heels, white kid gloves, and an aqua linen cambric handkerchief. He had his hair cut and was well dressed for a general appearance.

As the guests arrived in carriages at the front, the Victorian gentleman procured the lady and assisted her in descending the steps. He then conducted her to the lady's dressing room, leaving her in charge of the maid,

Dora, while he went to the gentleman's apartments to divest himself of his overcoat, hat, and boots.

After arranging her Victorian dress from the ride, the ladies retired to the ladies' room or awaited the gentleman's arrival at the dressing room door. Jane had a cloakroom where the ladies could give their shawls or cloaks to one of the maids. Dora and Joan were on hand to assist the ladies with any necessity the ladies may require, from arranging their hair to repairing a torn dress. Jane had Dora put several mirrors with a supply of hairpins, needles and threads, pins, and similar trifles around the room. When the gentleman returned, he took his lady's arm, led her into the ballroom, and conducted her to a seat next to him.

When Pam arrived at the top of the stairs, Joe was standing at the bottom of the stairs waiting. Finally, he took her arm and escorted her into the beautiful ballroom after she descended. She wanted to be the last to enter so all her friends would see her when they called her name. As the guests arrived, the floor managers gave the order for the orchestra to play.

As Joe and Pam entered the ballroom, Joe's first duty was to procure a program for Pam and introduce her to his friends. His friends would then place their names on her card to engage in dances. If Pam didn't want to dance with any of them, she took her little book out and told him that her dance card was full.

Joe and Pam were sitting talking to their friends when a trumpet signaled the assembly to take their positions on the floor for dancing. Joe danced the first set with Pam. Then he exchanged partners with a friend. Pam's father, Bill, was the Master Of The House and ensured that all the ladies danced. He noted which ladies appeared to be wallflowers and saw that they received an invitation to dance. He did this wholly unnoticed so that he didn't wound the self-esteem of the young ladies. Any gentleman he requested to dance with these ladies would be ready to accede to his wishes and even appear pleased at dancing with the lady he recommended. These young men rarely brought ladies with them and constantly bothered friends and floor managers by introducing them to the best dancers and the prettiest young ladies they saw in the room. If there were not as many gentlemen as ladies present, two ladies were permitted to dance together to fill up a set, or two gentlemen could dance if there were a shortage of ladies.

Joe asked Pam to dance and lightly touched her waist with his open palm as they walked to the floor. Joe was a great dancer and led Pam through the quadrille. Joe and Pam passed the night away dancing polkas, waltzes, and quadrilles. Pam and Joe walked around sipping drinks, nibbling delicacies from the finger buffet, and posing for professional photographs.

Joe and Pam were excited to do the Circassian Circle dance. Everyone came to the dance floor. They made two circles, one on the inside and the outside. When the music started to play, the men had their partners on their right-hand side. Along with everyone else in the circle, Joe and Pam joined hands to begin the dance. When the music started, everyone danced towards the middle for four steps and then back out for four steps, and then they repeated the steps.

The song leader told them, "Drop your hands, and ladies only, dance in for four, clap your hands with your partners, and out for four steps." Then he said, "Men only, dance in for four, and clap. Men stay in the middle and turn to face your partners." Everyone stayed with their partner and swung their partner by the right hand. Joe and Pam were having a great time.

The song leader told the couples to face anti-clockwise around the circle and join hands using a promenade hold (hold both hands across the front). Then the man held hands with his partner, and all the couples promenaded around the circle together. Then they reformed into a large circle and joined hands, ready to start the dance again.

Pam was out of breath and needed to sit down and have a drink. Pam saw some of her friends and told Joe to come over and meet them. Her friends Ben and Sally had been married for two years and hadn't seen Pam since their wedding. Sally told Pam they had a little girl named Mary Elizabeth.

Joe asked Pam, "Do you want to walk down by the river? We may get a better view of the mountains from there."

"Sure," Pam told him. She felt like she needed some air. She loved to be with Joe. They picked their way along the path of bare earth by the back steps. At one place, where a stream washed out their course, Pam took off her shoes, raised her dress in the front, put her hand out for Joe, and jumped. Joe held her hand as they walked. When they reached where a fallen tree blocked their path, he pulled her down and kissed her madly.

Joe unbuttoned her dress in front and held her breasts in his hands. After a few minutes, Pam buttoned her skirt up, fixed her hair, and told Joe, "We have to get back to the dining room for the banquet." Joe pulled her back in his arms and gave her one more kiss before returning.

As Joe looked down at Pam, he remembered the little details of when they met. He noticed her and her dad shortly after arriving at a restaurant. He was standing at the counter, immersed in a chart. When he looked up, he saw them at a corner table. He thought this woman was the most beautiful woman he had ever seen. He didn't know what to do; he walked over to the bar and looked first to their left and then to their right; he wanted to meet her. Joe knew her father from hunting. Her father was looking at her as he talked to her.

Joe thought they must be talking about something important as they leaned toward each other. As Joe walked towards their table, they continued to hold each other's hands. As he came near their table and smiled, they both looked up at him and returned his smile, doubling his investment.

Pam's father looked up at him when he stopped before them and asked, "Can I help you, son?"

They were studying Joe's face as they gave him their attention. As Joe stood there, he saw the abounding love and evident comfort between Pam and her father. That was something he hadn't seen in a long time.

Pam looked at her father; she looked more beautiful and innocent as she looked back up at Joe. There was something that attracted them to each other when they met. At least, that's how the story unfolded in Joe's mind as he looked at her. You can see a lot when you look at someone for the first time.

He looked over at her father and said, "Hello, Bill."

He told him he was ready to go hunting with him again. By invited him to sit with them. He was so excited. As they talked, he and Pam realized they were both born and brought up in Vicksburg. Even though they grew up in the same place, their paths never crossed. Both of their families owned plantations.

The next day, he saw her across the street by a window. She was in this lovely store, standing at the window, shopping. She looked so sweet and innocent. Joe watched her from his office. He had to meet her again, and as fate had it, her father came to his office to ask If he wanted to go hunting with him.

It was true romance for both of them; they were like two happy kids. They sat for hours by the river and watched the sunset go down, knowing they were creating more memories as they went along. As he kissed Pam under the moonlight, Joe realized that love was a powerful emotion. Rarely had a woman caught his heart and had him fall in love like his beauty Pam had.

CHAPTER THREE

THE FORMAL DINNER

Two days earlier, Jane had her husband, Jim, and the other slave men cleaning the larger dining room and getting ready for the banquet dinner for 100 guests. First, Jim and the men swept and mopped the floors and cleaned the windows. Next, drapes had to go up, rugs put on the floor, and round tables had to be brought in, with six chairs for each table. Jim knew it would take two days of working many hours to complete it. The men worked hard, but the dining room was ready for Dora, Joan, and Jane to set the table after two days.

Jane knew that the Victorian-era dinner party reflected the values of a progressive society, emphasizing etiquette and proper conduct. Hosting a dinner party allowed a Victorian woman to showcase her credentials in etiquette because a successfully planned and executed event helped her assert her position in upper-class society. In addition, Jane knew this banquet dinner was important; it would announce Joe and Pam's wedding day.

At the heart of the dinner party was the proper set Victorian table for Joe and Pam. The individual place settings contained pieces of silver to accommodate elaborate menus, often consisting of up to 12 courses. Joe and Pam's families would be at the front table. Around them were round tables to seat six guests at each table.

Jane had Dora and Joan put out the best table linens.

"During the mid-1800s", Jane told them, "it is not uncommon to use two or three layers of cloth that will be removed after subsequent courses are served."

Next, Jane showed Dora and Joan how to place the settings with the dinner plates at the center. She had them put the forks on the left side of the plates, starting with the dinner fork, followed by the fish fork and salad fork, and ending with a cocktail fork, which can also be on the other side of the plate following the spoons. Next, Jane, Dora, and Joan placed the bread with a folded napkin to the left of the dinner plate and forks because bread and butter plates were not part of a Victorian setting. Next, Joan placed crystal stemware right of the dinner plate. Finally, Joan placed a water goblet an inch above the dinner knife with the assorted wine, sherry, and champagne glasses to the right of the water glass in an ascending diagonal row or two. Of course, the placement depended on what was served. Jane checked to make sure Joan did everything right when she was finished.

When they finished setting the tables, they placed menu cards so that there was one for every two guests so that guests could pick and choose the menu items they wanted to eat. Name cards also appeared beside each guest's plate. Finally, they placed bowls of flowers on beveled mirrors on each table.

Jane told Joan and Dora, "Make sure the centerpieces do not interfere with conversation or block guests from being able to see one another across the tables."

After dinner, the women would retire to the drawing room for coffee or tea while the men remained behind in the dining room to smoke and drink port wine. Jane ensured the ladies had a place to sit and have everything they needed to enjoy coffee, tea, and tiny tea cakes.

After the dance, everyone went to the dining room to sit by their name card. Pam's father, Bill, and Joe had gone over the name list to ensure everyone was happy where they sat. Joe walked Pam into the dining room, pulled her chair out to be seated, and then sat down. Pam's dad, Bill, sat on the other side of Pam.

After all the guests found their seats and ordered their food from the menu, Pam's father, Bill, stood up.

"Good afternoon, ladies and gentlemen! Thank you all for coming. For those who don't know, I would like to announce that I will be giving my daughter away in marriage to Joe. So it's my great pleasure and privilege to welcome Joe to my family and all of you today at this amazing venue, on such a glorious day, to celebrate the forthcoming marriage of Joe and my beautiful daughter Pam."

"We are incredibly grateful for all of you coming here today to be part of this exceptional occasion, especially those who have traveled great distances. Pam is my only daughter, so this is the only chance I'll have to make a father-of-the-bride speech. So, naturally, over the years, I've spent quite a lot of time thinking about exactly what I want to say when this moment arrived. But then, last night, I was chatting with Pam, and she said, 'Dad, you can say whatever you like about me in your speech; just don't embarrass me. So, I had to rip the whole thing up and start again. I wrote what I wanted to say this morning, so I hope it works out okay."

"I want to start with how these two met at a dinner I hosted. As Pam and I talked in a restaurant, a young man watched my daughter from another table; he never took his eyes off her. After a while, he stood up, came over, introduced himself and started talking to me. I couldn't believe it. I wondered why he was telling me his name. I already knew him."

Pam's father told her, "Pam. You look stunning today; I'm certain we'd all agree. But beauty is only one of Pam's many attributes; she is fiercely loyal, dependable, fun-loving, and friendly. All of which, I'm certain, will make her a perfect partner to Joe."

"Joe, I think you are a fortunate man. I will also say that Pam is quite 'low maintenance,' another great attribute; she is easily pleased and doesn't hanker after the most expensive things. But that was obviously before this party, and the wedding preparations began. So, I'm now probably going to have to rethink that one. She is a perfect young lady whom I am immensely proud to have as my daughter, and I'm sure Joe will also be equally proud to call her his wife. At this point, I think it's also traditional to extol the virtues and intelligence of the groom, and I have copious notes. But I'm sorry, Joe, I just can't read your writing." Everyone laughed.

"I'll never forget that day sixteen months ago when I got a message from Joe saying he needed to speak to me. We were about to go on a hunting trip together, so I assumed he wanted advice on what type of gun to take. But instead, I am completely stunned when he hands me a letter asking for my permission to marry Pam."

"Afterwards, when we were hunting, I asked him what his Plan B was in case I said no. He didn't have one! So that was a bit disappointing; he's normally better prepared than that." Everyone laughed.

"I have known Joe for several years, and I've come to know him well. He's a great credit to his parents and family, and I genuinely can't think of a better person for my daughter. So, ladies and gentlemen, I am incredibly pleased to propose the first toast to the happy couple. Pam and Joe, here we are to a long and wonderful life together. To Pam and Joe." Everyone raised their glasses and toasted the couple with laughter and clapping.

Everyone was excited as their dinner was brought out by Joan, Dora, and Jane. Everyone talked to the couple and told them about their weddings and married lives. At the end of the dinner, everyone told the couple they had a great time and hugged Pam and Joe on the way out. Jim brought everyone's carriage up to them out front and helped them in.

Pam and Joe had a great time, but we're ready for some quiet time together. So Joe helped Pam up in his carriage and rode down to the river towards town to watch the steamboats. There was a stool for two by the river, and Joe and Pam sat down in the beautiful calm night, reliving the night.

The next day Pam and Joe went to a wedding store and had thank you cards made up to send to all their guests. The cards say, "To our family and friends...It meant the world to us to have you at our wedding announcement. Love and Laughter. You have contributed to our lives. You are all the ones we lean on, our partners in crime and our favorite people in the world. We hope you enjoyed the night's celebration and those we'll share for years: love, the newlyweds-to-be, Pam, and Joe.

CHAPTER FOUR

JANE'S MAMA'S BIRTHDAY

Jane's mama was from Vicksburg, Mississippi. Her mama, Helen, and Jane were sold on the auction block to different people. Jane thought about her mammy, who was still in Vicksburg. Jane missed her mammy and her brother Jerry. Jane had been in Natchez for over eight years since Master Jenkins bought her and moved here to live near his family.

Jane was the most pleasant person. She was always in the middle of everything in Natchez, taking Dora with her. Jane loved to go to every wedding reception and every baby shower. She was right there when the other ladies planned, organized, and ensured the occasions were done right. There were so many details for Jane to take care of. That's how the intelligent people of Natchez got to know her. She began to think of Natchez as her home more than Vicksburg.

Jane told Jim she needed to go and see her mammy. Her birthday was in a few days.

"Maybe Master Joe will take you," Jim said. "Maybe he will have to go to Vicksburg for some reason and let you go with him for the day. He likes to get up there every few months, and he hasn't gone for a while, so he is long overdue."

The last time Jane saw her mammy, she was told about when she was a six-month-old baby. Her mammy said they had put her in a little wood box by the fire to keep her warm. Her mammy said it was cold at night, and the wind howled outside. Jane's daddy, Paul, and her mama had watched over Jane with an eagle eye. She was their firstborn, and they couldn't stand to think they would lose her.

"I knew you would make it," her mammy told her." I had plenty of milk, and I often noticed you were hungry. I had to work in the kitchen of Master Ben, but he couldn't make me leave you, a tiny scrap of a baby as you were, so I brought your box into the big house and kept you in the kitchen while I cooked. Your daddy was still here with us then. Your daddy and I were happy once we saw that you would grow and plump up like a regular baby, only a bit smaller than most."

One day, when Master Joe was in the kitchen, Jane asked Master Jenkins about going with him to Vicksburg.

He told her, "I am going next week, and I will take you for the day. I have to talk to three different men about working for me."

When Jane returned to the cabin, she couldn't wait to tell Jim. She would bake her mammy a birthday cake and something to eat for her birthday. Jane found birthday candles in the kitchen drawer from a party she had done for Master Jenkins. He told her she could have them.

The night before she left, Jane told Dora to bring her a warm brick and take it over to her bed for her and Jim to keep warm for the night. It was freezing in their small cabin, and Jane pulled the quilt one way and the top blanket the other way, then brushed it smooth. Dust and leaves had blown in with the wind when the door blew open. Jane's feet were hurting, and she took her shoes off and set them along the back wall of their shack. Then, she went to bed with Jim with the warm brick at their feet for the night. She rolled onto her side, pulling the quilt tight on her and Jim. She thought about the free people of Natchez and hoped one day it would be her and her family. Jane couldn't sleep. She was too excited that she was going to spend her mama's birthday with her.

In the summer, Jim, Jane, and Dora worked in the backyard in a big garden with rows of beans, peas, and corn. Joan had a little cabin with a small bed next to them. Jane showed Dora and Joan how to wash the only dress they had to wear daily in the wash pan, using a rubboard, and hanging the underclothing every night to dry by the following day.

Many new enslaved people lived in tents, but Master Jenkins had Jim and some more enslaved people build a one-room cabin for Jim and his family. Jane was unsure where all the new enslaved people came from or how long they would be there. One day she went out and introduced herself to some of the new slaves. She wanted them to know they could rely on her to help in any way she could.

Jane knew Dora and Joan needed to settle down, but there was not a suitable single man among the freemen in Natchez. The only young men they ran into at Master Jenkins' home were enslaved, not free. Jane wanted Dora to marry a free man. Jane wished she, Joan, and Dora had a better place to live than the shack. But Jim kept telling her she was lucky it was not the barn.

Joan and Dora knew how to work. They could lift, hammer, and carry wood for the fire better than most men. Master Jenkins had them in the cotton fields, nailing boards on the home, cooking, and lots more. Jane thought any man would be lucky to get either of them as a wife.`

Dora walked around in the kitchen, looking for her mama. Jane was not there, but the fire was still going. Jane probably had gone into the big house to clean the bedrooms after all the guests had left the party. Dora sat down and folded her arms on the table. The warmth in the room washed over her, and suddenly, all she wanted to do was sleep. She rested her head on her arms. The fire made little popping sounds, and then she was asleep, caught in the snare of a dream. She immediately sees a woman standing behind a window; the glass is washed with rain, and there are children in front of the woman sitting at desks.

Suddenly, she was startled awake, but the dream was gone, and the only sound she heard was her mammy Jane telling her, "We have work to do. The ballroom and dining room still need to be cleaned, and dishes washed and put away."

Dora was tired; she taught some small slave children how to read and do math in her off time. She took off her jacket, tossed it on the chest next to her bed, and put on her work clothes. She wished she could sleep for an hour, but she knew her mama, Jane, would come to get her and would not be happy doing it.

When Dora arrived back at the big house she and Joan started washing dishes and cleaning all the tables. Over a hundred guests had been at the party, and everything still had to be cleaned up before Master Jenkins and Miss Pam returned from camping. Joe and Pam wanted to get away for three days on a hunting and camping trip and have some time to relax.

Jim took the tables back to the shed after Joan and Dora removed the dishes, tablecloths, and food. The ballroom and dining room were clean. Extraordinarily little food was left to be put away. So the kitchen staff got to carry some food home to their families.

As Joan and Dora were washing dishes, Jane was starting dinner. "Master Jenkins will take me to see my mammy on her birthday next week." She told them, "I need you to help me make a birthday cake and a meal to take with me."

Dora walked to the pantry and pulled out everything she needed for the cake. She mixed all the ingredients and put the cake in the oven.

Joe and Pam had a great time camping. Joe loaded the wagon with bedrolls, tin coffee pots, dishes, food, and blankets. He had Jane fix him and Pam some food to take to cook over a campfire. Pam had never been camping, but Joe made it sound fun, and they would enjoy time with their friends. They went camping by a lake. They both loved to fish and took fishing poles with them.

When Joe and Pam got to the lake in the woods, four of their friends were already there. Joe helped Pam out of the wagon, and they started getting their camp ready. Joe built a fire; the sparks were flying in the air as Joe and Pam sat down cozy next to each other. Joe was cooking their supper over the fire and making coffee.

Earlier, Joe had set up a tent for him and his best man; it overlooked the lake and hills. Wildflowers were growing everywhere. Joe and Pam walked through the woods picking flowers with two of their friends, and as Joe handed her one, he kissed her.

As they slowly walked back to the fire, Joe kissed her again. The tents were up, the fire was bright, and dinner was made. As Joe and Pam sat up against a log eating, they talked about all the beautiful things they would do after the wedding with their friends. Pam helped Joe wash the dishes, and they both went to their different tents for the night. Pam looked at the stars and lake before finally going into her tent. It was a beautiful romantic night; she hated for it to end.

The following day, while Pam was still asleep, Joe got up and cooked breakfast, and made coffee. The fire was blazing and warm. Joe went to Pam's tent and said, "Breakfast is ready."

Pam was sitting in her chair while the other lady was still asleep, and she looked up at Joe from her book with a smile. Joe went to the campfire, poured Pam a cup of hot coffee, brought it back to the tent, and handed it to her. Pam smiled at him as he sat by her looking out at the lake.

Joe got their fishing poles and baited Pam's hook for her, and together they caught six fish for their supper. Joe cleaned the fish as Pam got the pan out to cook. As Pam was cooking the fish, Joe approached her and placed his arms around her neck. They sat together and watched the sun go down over the lake as the fire blazed brightly. Joe promised they would do it again very soon.

As they ate, Joe and Pam enjoyed their friends all sitting around the fire with them.

After everything was loaded and the fire put out, Joe helped Pam up in the wagon and told the horse, Star, "Let's go home."

It was late when Joe and Pam rode up to Pam's parent's house in town. Once they stopped, Joe helped Pam down, and she went into the house. After Joe rode home, Jim helped Joe unload the wagon and took the wagon, and Star, to the barn. Jane had supper ready for him and brought it all to the dining room after he sat down. It had been a wonderful camping trip for them, with four of their friends, and after supper, Joe walked out to the porch to sit in the dark. Joe was thinking of Pam and watching the stars in the sky.

On Monday morning, Master Jenkins was ready to go to town, and Jane was up. She cooked breakfast for Jim, fixed his lunch, kissed him goodbye, and wished him a good day. She was standing outside when Joe came out to the buggy. Joe helped Jane with the cake and food, and they left early to ride twelve miles to town. Joe had a big day; he had to find three enslaved people to buy, and he was taking Jane to see her mammy for the day. Jane wrote her mammy the week before and told her she was coming. Her mammy was watching out the window for Jane when they pulled up.

Joe pulled up at the back of Master Ben's home, helped Jane down, and carried her food inside. Joe told her, "I will be back in four hours to go home."

Helen hugged her daughter and told her she was glad to see her. Jane was excited to see her. She lit the candles on the cake and sang "Happy Birthday" to her mammy. Helen and Jane had a great time eating Jane's dinner. They sat in the living room, discussing everything they could think of. But four hours go by fast when you are having fun. Joe pulled up, and Jane hugged her mammy goodbye and promised to return soon. Twelve miles was a long ride home, but it gave Jane time to think about her wonderful time with her mammy.

Joe pulled up in front of his home and helped Jane down. "Did you have a great time?"

Jane grinned at him and told him, "It was the best time of my life."

Jane decided to go outside after lunch, meet some of the ladies in the tents, and take them a piece of cake she had made Master Jenkins and Pam. She walked over to two ladies and introduced herself. One lady's name was Sally, and the other one was Sue. Sally had two children, Joe and Sam, and Sue had a little girl, Jenny. Dora taught them in her class. Sally and Sue washed clothes in a big pot over a fire and hung them on a line. Jane told them she would help them while they got to know each other. After about an hour, Jane told them goodbye and asked them to come to see her for coffee sometime in the evening.

Sally and Sue told Jane they would bring their kids to Dora's school around three o'clock. Sally suggested to Jane, "Maybe we can get a break and have that coffee?"

Jane laughed and told them she would be waiting for them in the kitchen at three o'clock. At three, Sally and Sue brought their children to Dora's class, and the ladies all sat down in Master Jenkins' kitchen for cake and coffee for an hour. Master Jenkins didn't mind as long as Jane had her work done.

Sally and her family were bought by Master Jenkins from a slave trader two weeks earlier, and her husband Tom was working in the cotton field for Master Jenkins. Sally worked in the cotton fields chopping six days a week, but today was Sunday, and she was off to do her work around the tent. Sue and her family were bought one week ago, and she worked in the fields with her husband James every day but Sunday.

Sally was a dark-skinned lady weighing about one-twenty, and Sue was a more considerable lady weighing around one-forty. Both ladies were amiable and loved to talk. Their children were small and could ride on the cotton sacks with their parents pulling them. Tom and James were hard workers, and their wives had difficulty keeping up with them. Even though the ladies picked together, they knew not to talk much, or if they did, only in a whisper so Master Jenkins couldn't hear them. After selecting a row and a half, their sacks would be complete. They would load their bags across their shoulders, carry them upfront, weigh them on a scale, and write down the weight.

Enslaved people never got paid for their work. They just received a room and food to eat. Tom and James would pick around two hundred pounds daily, but the ladies had the children on their sacks, slowing them down. They would pick around one seventy a day.

Tom told everyone, "Let's take a five-minute break and get some water from the jug under the tree."

Everyone was hot from working in the hot sun all morning. Tom and James laid down on the ground to rest, but the ladies had to give the children water, and by the time Sally and Sue got a drink, it was time to go back to work.

Every enslaved person was tired and talked in low voices about how they wished they could be free. Master Joe never whipped them, but he wanted them to work hard and get the cotton done. Often, Master Joe would come out to the cotton fields and work with them.

At seven at night, everyone would drag themselves back to their cabin or their rooms in the basement. Jim and Tom had built a shower behind the houses for everyone to get cleaned up after their hard day of work. By the time the ladies had supper ready to eat and had washed the dishes everyone was ready to fall in their cots. Then they had to get up at 6 am. and do it all again.

CHAPTER FIVE

SEWING BY HAND

Clothing the family in 1858 was an important task, and most of the work was the responsibility of the women. On every stitch of Pam's clothes, the sewing had to be done by hand. Most of the time, by enslaved people.

Elias Howe invented the sewing machine in 1846, but most people couldn't afford to buy one. Nobody had the vast amount of clothes that we have today. They made do with one outfit for every day, one for Sunday best, and perhaps one other, or parts of another, for seasonal change. Even wealthy people like Pam didn't necessarily have lots of clothes. However, their money allowed them to purchase ready-made items from the storekeeper. More affluent people, like Pam, would have a live-in seamstress.

Where a family lived determined, to a great extent, where and how they obtained their clothing. Wealthy people ordered their clothes from New York City, and town dwellers usually purchased the fabrics or garments from specialty or general stores.

There was a great variety of fabrics available for making clothing in 1858. Wool and linen were the most common; cotton and silk were scarcer and more expensive. Hundreds of woven patterns were available for women to make family clothes. Women even made their husbands' clothes. A rich selection of colors existed even before synthetic dyes. Often, the entire family helped produce the cloth used for their clothing, especially if it was rural.

Silk was for wealthier people to own. It came from India or China. Men would have everyday clothing consisting of a linen pullover shirt, full sleeves, deep buttoned cuffs, a great collar, and exceptionally long tails to tuck into the trousers. When the sweater started getting old, a slave lady would mend it for him. Joe wore leather boots of various heights for daywear in the fields or slipper-like dancing shoes when he and Pam were dancing.

Joe was wealthy from his cotton. Sometimes, he would express his wealth by choosing more delicate fabrics and a more extensive and varied wardrobe. He wore cotton shirts and linen, ruffled at his neck and sleeves. Only wealthier men, like Joe, owned enough shirts to be able to set one or more shirts aside as nightshirts. Pam and other ladies wore simple day dresses for their home and farm work; they opened down the front to the waist. For many women, this was better to serve the needs of the nursing infant in the field. The dresses were pinned closed or fastened with hooks and eyes closely set. The sleeves were usually long; the fashion had most of the fullness extremely high early in the decade but lower in the arms as the year progressed. Pam's skirts were full; she wore them pleated or gathered onto the bodice. Pam was tall, so her waist was slightly higher than the natural waistline.

Joan and Dora washed and ironed the aprons for Pam. She wore them to protect her skirt during work and often wore dressy aprons at home. Pam often wore fashionable lightweight kid leather slippers, black every day, but pastel color to match her party dresses. Some of her shoes had ribbons on the front with her heels very low.

Pam had a great interest in fashion, and she ordered styles from London, Paris, and the Eastern cities. Monthly magazines detailed all the latest modes and fabrics. Pam wrote down all the descriptions to show her seamstress what she wanted to reflect in her dress.

During the Civil War, there were a lot of changes and adjustments. This altered and disrupted people's ways of life and, in some cases, was lost forever. Most women of the South felt this loss was against them. The wealthy women in the South liked going to tea parties and ball dances where enslaved people would wait on them. White elite men had power over women, lower-class whites, and enslaved people. The privileged Southern way of life and patriarchal dominance affected planter-class female perceptions about the war. It allowed them to step out of their socially defined gender prescriptions to support the Confederate Cause.

The war offered elite Confederate women the opportunity to be a part of the struggle for Southern independence and, like their men, define themselves as "independent" Southern women.

CHAPTER SIX

THE COURTSHIP

Joe had been courting Pam for over a year. He realized that he liked Pam from the minute he met her. Since he believed God was the one who planned their relationship, it was probably safe to assume that God had drawn Joe's heart towards Pam before either of them even realized it. He knew it wouldn't be long before he was engaged to Pam. Their courting was taken very seriously-- by both sides. Pam's mother groomed her for this role in life, her duty as a wife and a mother. Being trained, she learned to sing and play piano in church. Pam took dance lessons for the ballroom. She was able to be conversant about the light literature of the day. She also learned a different language. She had to complete her education and be officially available in the marriage court. She couldn't be married until she was eighteen. She always had a new wardrobe for the season, so she appeared her best in public for her suitor. Her father was her chaperone because Pam was someone never allowed out of the house by herself, especially in mixed company.

Joe first spoke to Pam at her father's table in a restaurant Bill walked out of the restaurant with them and never left his daughter's side. Joe knew he had to take care in the early stages of their courtship. By spring, he must have been thinking about her quite a bit because his mother asked him what he thought of Pam.

He told her that Pam was someone that he would consider marrying. He knew that after their conversation, he started thinking about the topic even more, and then by the middle of summer, he was optimistic that he wanted to marry Pam.

He was a gentleman and knew he couldn't automatically resume their acquaintance on the street. He had to be reintroduced by her father or a family friend. And then, only upon permission from Pam. Joe took Pam and her family to church suppers and holiday balls.

On Saturday, July 4th, Joe attended a birthday party for Pam, and after that, he decided that he was way too interested in Pam to keep being just a friend. On Tuesday of the following week, he asked her parents if he could talk with them about moving toward a courtship.

They joked as a family that they would put some names in a hat and pick one out when the time came. When they sat down to talk, Joe asked, If they could just put one word in the hat - HIS. After a few minutes, they decided that the cap wasn't necessary, and they spent the evening talking about how he would take care of Pam.

One day Pam was asked to come to help Joe on their farm for the day. She wanted to get to know him better. They wanted to pray about getting married.

Sunday morning, Joe picked Pam up for church and semi-accidentally ended up talking with Pam from when the service started until they had to leave. Then, Joe rode her home in the wagon. On Pam's second visit to the farm, Joe worked more closely with Pam as she helped him and his sibling to prune and tie up their tomato plants. Joe and Pam enjoyed the time with each other, and he continued to be impressed with her. The next evening, he talked to her parents again, and their conversation concluded that he had their blessing to court their daughter.

On a typical day, Pam rose at 11 a.m. and ate breakfast in her dressing room before her maid helped her dress. Pam's parents loved concerts and would take Pam with them. She loved music. Under the watchful eye of her father as her chaperone, Joe was invited to go. Their romance lasted, it was love at first sight, and within six months, they talked of marriage. However, Joe told her they should wait a year. He still had to speak to her father. He wanted to give her parents time to discover what kind of man he was. Joe worked hard in the fields and had one hundred and twenty-five enslaved people.

Joe and Pam loved to play bridge and would include their friends. At one of the parties at Pam's home, a stranger became attentive to Pam. Joe was a little jealous as he watched him. Joe walked over and asked Pam for a dance. She looked at her dance card and told him she would love to. Once they were on the dance floor, she thanked him for taking her away from the strange man.

Joe was nervous as he got dressed. He wrote her father a letter and asked for his consent for his daughter's hand in marriage. If her father refused, he knew the engagement couldn't happen. Joe prayed Bill would okay the wedding. He didn't know what he would do if her father said no. He didn't want Pam to marry someone else.

When Pam's father received the letter, he had been hunting with Joe and his family for a few years. He thought Joe wanted to know what kind of gun to bring for the hunt. Bill was surprised when he opened the letter. When Joe met him at the hunt, Bill asked Joe what his plan B was if he had said no. Joe said he didn't have one.

By the end of the year, their relationship had been cemented, with their eyes on the future. Marriage and a promising future were their goals! Pam was in an upper-class family, and in upper-class marriages, the wife often brought a generous dowry, an enticement for marriage.

One night Ben told Joe to come into his office. The financial aspects of their marriage were openly discussed. Bill wanted to know about Joe's fortune. He wanted to ensure Joe could care for her for years until death parted them. Joe knew he had to prove his worth in keeping Pam in the level of life she was accustomed to. In addition, he had to improve her social standing. Bill had studied Joe's bank account and approved the wedding. He stood up and shook Joe's hand. As he opened the door, he welcomed Joe to the family.

Joe walked Pam out to the river and told her 'the good news.' Pam was so excited and couldn't wait to write to all her friends about the news. Their engagement lasted a year before they started planning their wedding. Joe had finalized the engagement with a large stone ring. Now that they were engaged, Joe and Pam could be more intimate. They could stroll alone at night, hold hands in public, and take unchaperoned rides by the river. There was true romance and love during the year. Joe sent Pam flowers and letters almost every day, and Pam would spend hours writing him letters.

Pam's parents had a large dinner for the couple before the wedding. Joe invited the aunts, uncles, and cousins of both sides. Joe had Jane, Joan, and Dora set up the dining room with food for seventy-five family members.

Jane was busy in the kitchen telling everyone what to do and what tables to set up. Joan and Dora were to set all the tables and have everything ready for her to check the day before the family arrived. Joan and Dora did a great job with the dishes and went outside to cut roses for the tables. As they entered the back door, Jane cleaned a place off for them to cut the flowers. They placed them in vases, careful that they stood no more than three inches above the vase. They didn't want to block anyone's view while talking at the table.

On the eve of the dinner, the carriages started arriving. Jim and some other enslaved people were out front to help the ladies out and down the steps. All the women hugged each other and talked as they came up the steps to go inside to meet everyone. Joe was standing with his and Pam's parents greeting all the guests when they arrived.

The ladies were taken to the powder room to fix their hair and makeup. One of the slave women was there to help with their dresses. The men waited outside the door for their lady.

Joe waited at the bottom of the stairs for Pam's entrance. Everyone was looking at the couple as he took Pam's arm and brought her into the dining room. The food looked delicious. Jane had outdone herself. Ham, turkey, steak, and more were on the buffet. Enslaved men were walking around with drinks on a tray.

Pam was showered with gifts for her and Joe. After dinner, Joe and Pam sat at the table and opened the beautiful gifts for their home. They hugged everyone and thanked them for their assistance and for coming.

Pam hugged her father and mother as the last guest left and told them how much she loved them. Joe had to work in the field the next day and told Pam he loved her before giving her a night kiss.

CHAPTER SEVEN

MAKING OF THE WEDDING DRESS

Pam and Joe had many things to get ready for. The wedding day was just four months away. This was the most important event in a Victorian girl's life. It was the day Pam's mother had prepared her for from the moment she was born. Pam knew no other ambition. She would marry Joe, and she would marry well.

Pam and her mother knew there was lots of work for the wedding and everything leading up to it. So Pam had chosen the month and day of her wedding. June was the most popular month, for June was named after Jono, the Roman Goddess of Marriage. This month was supposed to bring prosperity and happiness to all who wed in this month. If married in June, Pam would likely give birth to her first child in spring.

Pam wanted a white silk wedding dress. However, brides had not always worn white for their marriage ceremony. In the 16th and 17th centuries, Pam knew girls in their teens married in pale green, a sign of fertility. At the same time, a mature girl in her twenties wore a brown dress.

Pam loved the Queen Victoria wedding dress in 1840 and wanted one made just like it. Pam wanted her dress with a fitted bodice, a tiny waist, and a full skirt (over hoops and petticoats). She wanted it made of organdy, tulle, lace, gauze, and silk. Her veil would be made with lace. Pam wanted six bridesmaids; their dresses would be white with covers. The shrouds would be attached to a coronet of flowers with orange blossoms in their hair. Pam would have everyone in their wedding party wearing short white kid gloves, hankies embroidered with her maiden name initials, silk stockings embroidered up the front, and flat shoes decorated with bows or ribbons on the instep. Pam had a picture of Queen Victoria in her wedding gown and wanted Betty, her seamstress, to make her dress.

On Monday morning, Pam and her mother, June, had the carriage and horse brought around to the front. Both walked out of the home arm and arm with beautiful dresses and matching hats. Each woman carried a parasol to cover their head and shade them from the sun. Jim helped them into the carriage and sat on the top seat, ready to take them to town. This was a big day for Pam. They had a lot to do to prepare before the wedding. Pam's mother took Pam's hands in hers and smiled at her. They were both excited and couldn't wait to pick out the fabric for Pam's dress.

Betty knew they were coming and had picked out ten different rolls of fabric for Pam. Jim had pulled the carriage in front of Betty's shop and helped the ladies down. They were like two schoolgirls laughing and talking as they entered the shop. Betty came and hugged them with a smile on her face. Pam looked at all the fabric and told Betty everything she wanted. Betty was going to be busy for the next four months with a wedding dress, six bridesmaids' dresses, two little girls' dresses, and Pam's mom's dress. She had to work day and night to finish on time.

Once the ladies had everything picked out, they hugged Betty bye. Following were shoes to match. As they walked two doors down to the next store, they looked in the windows as they passed. As they walked into Josh's shoe store, Mr. Josh was waiting on a lady. He told them to look around, and he would be right with them.

Pam picked out some beautiful shoes for herself and her mother, June. When Mr. Josh finished with his customer, he helped them try on the shoes. Unfortunately, the first ones Pam tried on didn't fit, so Mr. Josh got another size, which fit perfectly.

Pam had to return for a dress fitting Friday morning, and she was supposed to bring her bridesmaids and the two little girls for fitting for their dresses and shoes. While Pam was getting shoes, she picked up gloves for everyone but Joe.

Her mother reminded her that they must get the invitations done, and she had a friend that did excellent work. So, as Jim waited in the carriage seat, Pam and June walked across the street to Mrs. Betsy's Wedding Shop.

The date was set, and Pam had to pick out the invitations carefully. Pam discovered that picking out the perfect wedding stationery isn't as simple as couples imagined. Mrs. Betsy was there to help her. She showed her paper types, font, theme, sizing, inserts, and cost; it was a lot to think about. But Betsy and Pam's mother were both a great help. First, they picked out the shapes and sizes. Pam wanted them vintage but elegant. It was going to be a formal wedding. Finally, they picked out invitations with flowers at the top and bottom.

The invitations read, "You are invited to the wedding of Pam Hook and Joe Jenkins, June 24th, 1860, at four o'clock on Court Street, Jenkin's Plantation. Dinner and dancing to follow." Pam told Betsy to make two hundred invitations and asked when they would be ready. Betsy told her by Friday when she came in for her fitting.

Pam and her mother were ready for lunch and wanted to go to The Sephora Restaurant for a great meal. The hostess seated them as soon as they walked in. The tables were beautifully set. The waiter came over to take their order, and Pam wanted the lemony Chicken Saltimbocca. This was her favorite. An Italian-inspired dish that combined tender chicken, woodsy sage, bright lemon, and salty prosciutto into one delectable dish was served with wine and coffee.

Her mother, June, ordered Steakhouse Beef and Pepper. The crisp and colorful peppers on top of beef sirloin strips were seasoned in a sauce and served with wine and then coffee. The steakhouse was beautiful, and the food was excellent.

Pam asked for a quiet table so she and her mother could talk and plan the wedding. The waiter brought their food out fast and made sure he waited on them often. Finally, after two hours of sitting and planning the wedding, Pam and June were ready to return to the carriage and go home. Jim was waiting by the trees and saw them coming down the street with many bags. He took the bags, loaded everything in the carriage, and then helped the ladies inside and closed the door.

The wedding was being held in Pam and Joe's church. Pam told Betty her dress must have a train with a veil of the same length, and her cloak had to cover her face. Joe wasn't to lift it until after the ceremony. Pam's mother gave Pam her pearls to wear. Pam thought, "I need something old, something new, something borrowed, something blue, and a lucky sixpence in my shoe." As she went down the list, her mother's pearls were old, something new was her wedding dress, Joe had his mother's embroidered handkerchief, and she still needed something blue. Her friend gave her a blue garter for something blue; then, she had the list finished.

Pam's best friend had two little girls and a little boy. The little girls were the flower girls, and the little boy was to carry the rings. Pam and her friend, May, we're going over the style of dresses for the girls. Their dresses, she told Betty, should be white muslin tied with a ribbon sash that matched their shoes and stockings. The dresses must be long.

Pam and May went shopping Tuesday morning for May's son, John's clothing for the wedding. They got him a velvet jacket, short trousers, and round linen collars fastened by a large bowl of white crepe de chine. He got black-laced shoes with buckles and a white silk hose. They decided his velvet suit would be black with a matching hat. His hat would be removed for the church ceremony.

Pam, her mother, June, and May only had four months to prepare everything. Joe's slave maids and Pam's maid did all the cooking and set up the tables. Joe had flowers all over the plantation that he planned to put in vases for the tables, but Pam wanted to leave them alone and ordered flowers.

CHAPTER EIGHT

PAM'S TRIP

Pam woke up in a nice fantastic bed. The breeze was blowing across her. Pam was thinking about how cozy this was and how she couldn't wait to be Joe's bride. She told Joe last night, "Remember that I will be going to see my father and mother at their estate in Vicksburg. I am leaving in the morning on the stagecoach."

Even though she didn't want to, Pam climbed out of bed, went to her dresser, removed her underclothes, and headed for the bathroom. Joe would be there soon.

When Joe arrived he carried Pam's luggage and put it in the back of the carriage before helping Pam into the seat. It was a nice warm day, and they enjoyed the blue sky as they rode. The stagecoach arrived on time. Joe helped Pam down from the carriage, removed her luggage, and handed it to the coachman as he came around and opened the door for Pam. Joe kissed Pam bye before he helped her up onto the stage and closed the door. He told her he would see her in two weeks and asked her to hurry back home. As the stagecoach left down the road, Joe waved bye and watched until she was gone.

It was a thirty-mile trip to the hotel where Pam spent the night before carrying on the following day. When they reached the hotel, a man took Pam's bag inside. A lady at the desk checked her in.

"The room is at the top of the stairs on the left," she said.

Pam walked up the stairs and into her room. It was a genuinely lovely room with a single bed, a dresser, and a pitcher of water with a water bowl to freshen up. Pam was very tired from the stage ride and after having supper downstairs she couldn't wait to get into bed.

The following day, the carriage stopped at the stagecoach depot in Vicksburg, Mississippi. A couple of moments later, the coachman came and opened the door. The trip had been long and dusty, and as Pam stepped down, the warm spring air brushed her face with dust as the coachman helped her and another lady out. Pam opened her parasol and placed it over her head, shielding herself from the intense rays of the morning sun.

She expected her father and mother to be there any moment to pick her up, but even a short time in direct sunlight would make Pam's delicate cream skin burn. She managed to stay out of the sun during the stagecoach ride; she didn't plan to ruin her appearance now that the ride was over. She wanted to look great for her mamma.

Some young man came up to her. "Can I have your luggage delivered somewhere, Miss?"

She shook her head no. "You can leave my bags beside me. My father and mother will be here soon to pick me up."

The man grinned at her. "Who's your father and mother, if you don't mind me asking?"

Pam pressed her lips together. She supposed it didn't matter if she told the man. Everyone in the small town would know her parents and soon enough of her arrival. "Bill and June Hook."

"I know your whole family. That means you're cousins with Judy and Jean Hook. I went to school with both. They're good people." Pam was lucky to have such a wonderful family, and she knew it. "How long will you be staying," he wanted to know.

"I am just staying for two weeks; my future husband is waiting for me back in my hometown." As she looked up the street, she was relieved to hear the familiar voice of her father coming toward her.

"I can't believe my eyes. I barely recognized you, Pam," her father said. She turned to the side to find her father and mother standing next to a tall, dark-haired man. She assumed it was Jean's husband, Jimmy.

"We're so glad you're here," her mother said as she reached out and pulled her daughter into an embrace. "I see the Hook's fair complexion remains; you could pass for your cousin Judy."

"How is Joe doing?" her mother asked. "I bet he is missing you already," she said as they walked to the carriage where her father helped both of them in.

As Pam's father helped her into the carriage, Pam asked," How's my brother Jack doing?"

"He is well, as is my mother. They send their love to all of you," her mother said. "They wished they could have come with me, but my father is busy building the new steamboat."

"The day is getting away from us; we need to head home," Bill said as he and the young man helped get Pam's luggage loaded into the wagon.

"Where's the rest of the family?" Pam inquired as the men made short work of loading her luggage. She had hoped her other four cousins would have come to meet her.

"They're at home waiting for us and will be ready to eat. They wanted to come, but it would have been complete chaos with the children. So we are all you get," her father laughed and took up the reins.

It was five miles from town to the Hook's plantation. As Ben pulled up, Pam's cousins and their children ran out to meet them. Her cousin Judy grabbed her and talked non-stop as they walked up the steps.

CHAPTER NINE

TRIP TO VICKSBURG, MISSISSIPPI

Pam was relieved she had something to distract her from missing Joe. She and her dad enjoyed the dinner with family and friends, but Pam was glad when it was over. She was tired from a long day and was ready to sleep.

The next morning her mother told her the mayor decided to host a social in the town square. The social event was a fun way to keep her mind off Joe and give her a much-needed rest from the wedding plans. She went back to her room and started to get ready. She had her mama's slave help her get dressed and placed the final pin in her hair to secure her curls.

"There is a picnic in the afternoon and a dance in the evening. That means it will be a long event," her cousin told her.

Pam wanted to make sure her curls held up for the entire night. Once she was certain they would not fall, she inspected her red satin dress for a final time in the mirror. It was her best dress, and she always looked great in it. She added a set of earrings and a necklace.

When she came down the stairs, her mother was sitting in the parlor. "You look beautiful," she said as Pam reached out and gently hugged her. "I wish Joe could see you right now."

Pam's cousin Judy came up behind them, "Are you both ready?"

"We are," June said, picking up her shawl from the chair and handing it to Pam. "I'm looking forward to a nice day with my family and friends."

"Me, too," Judy said with a smile as she stepped out of the way to let Pam and her mother pass through the door. "It's been a long time since the town has had something to celebrate. We are excited Pam gets to attend a town social with us. I can't wait to introduce her to every one of our friends."

The cool wind was blowing, and Pam pulled her shawl tightly around her chest as she stepped up into the carriage and moved over for Judy and her mother, June.

Pam looked around her parents' home before they rode down the road. The house had been owned and operated by the Hooks for several generations, but recently they had to take on farmers. Sharing the profits by buying slaves to keep from losing their land was not uncommon for folks at this time, but it was difficult. Pam didn't want to burden her family, but her parents wanted to give her and Joe a big wedding. The women stepped out of the carriage with the help of the men.

John told Judy, "Did I tell you how pretty you look in that dress?" He reached out to take Judy's hand and placed it in the crook of his arm, walking to the dance.

"You say that every time I wear this dress, which is a lot since we can't afford to buy new ones." She reached up and kissed him with a thank you smile.

"You can always borrow one of mine; they will be new to you," Pam told her.

Judy smiled at Pam and told her, "I would love it, but I may ruin it."

"I wouldn't worry about that; I can have it cleaned. You are welcome to any one I have."

John and Judy had a secret they hadn't shared with the family.

Pam's father looked at her and said," Is there something wrong, Judy? You look like you aren't feeling well."

Judy shook her head before she glanced over at John with a smile.

"Are you all blind?" Jean asked. Judy has been ill regularly lately, and her clothes aren't fitting like they used to. It's obvious; Judy's going to have a baby."

Pam's mother was so excited she clapped her hands. "You are? I can't believe it."

"I wanted to tell you," said Judy, "but I wasn't sure how it was going to go."

Judy's father and mother were standing by Judy. Her father couldn't believe it, "I'm going to be a grandfather. It seems you're keeping up on your end of the deal, John," he said coming over and patting the young man on the back.

Jean was jumping up and down, "I am going to be an Aunt Jean. I can't way to babysit and make her clothes if it is a girl."

"We didn't want to make an announcement quite yet," Judy said.

Judy's mother wanted to tell the world she would be a grandmother, but Judy wanted her to wait.

Her cousin Jean told her, "This is my first time getting to be an aunt, and she doesn't want us to run and tell everyone."

"There'll be plenty of time for that down the road. Let's make it the Hooks family secret," Judy told them.

"Congratulations," Pam hugged Judy and John's necks. "That's wonderful news."

A lot of families were already at the town square when they arrived. Everyone was setting up for the picnic. There were over a hundred tables with chairs, but only a few left when they strolled up. Pam didn't see anyone she knew, but that was not surprising since it had been six years since the last summer she spent in Vicksburg.

"Let's put the blankets on the grass for the children to sit and put the picnic baskets on the table," Ben suggested.

Everywhere you looked, there were games for everyone, and all the children that had come wanted to hurry and eat so they could play. No one could wait to do the cakewalk; there were two tables of cakes, cookies, pies, and more. Pam and Jean got to the cakewalk first. Then, the music started, and John, Bill, and June jumped in on numbers. They were all laughing and having fun. Jean won the first cake, then June. Before everyone quit, John, Pam, and Bill all had a cake or cookies.

Bill asked, "What in the world are we going to do with all this dessert?" Everyone came back to the table to eat the food.

All the women started serving the children first; then the men joined in on the fried chicken, potato salad, baked beans, homegrown tomatoes, and don't forget all the dessert.

Two hours later everyone was ready for a swim in the lake. Kids started running to see who would get there first, but the men told them they couldn't go in until everyone was there to watch them. Kids were having a great time splashing and dunking each other and playing with a ball. Some of them saw a log floating in the water and started to jump on it. The log rolled over, and the kids fell off. One of them got back on and started walking and dancing on the log. It was a great day for every child as they laughed and played in the water. You could hear a man rowing his boat nearby as the children played in waves that crashed on the bank. A flock of seagulls flew by, and the children ran to get bread to feed them.

Judy didn't want to swim, so she volunteered to do magic tricks.

"How about a little fun with money?" she asked the kids.

They couldn't believe it when she pulled a coin from behind one of their ears. Next, she showed them how to put a coin on their elbow and then catch it in their hands. She showed them several tricks before teaching them how to perform each one. They must have practiced for a couple of hours. They all wanted to master the tricks, so they could show their dads when they got home. There were going to be a lot of kids digging in couches, looking for a change that night.

All the men and boys got in a three-legged race. There were twenty-six men and boys in the race. It was the funniest thing you ever saw. Everyone was running and falling, but finally, they had a winner. John and his son, Mark, ran over the finish line first and won a fishing pole each. It forced them to work together in a silly way. But by the end, they were laughing and joking with each other without even realizing it. Their mood towards each other had flipped, and they made sure to point out how well they worked together.

All the ladies in town had baked cherry pies for the pie-eating contest. There had to be sixty pies total for the contest. Every lady in town had been making cherry pies all week to ensure there would be enough. It wasn't a picnic without a pie-eating contest.

All the men and boys got set up behind tables to be ready for the contest. Everyone sat in front of a pie, and when the gun went off, the pie-eating group put their faces in the pie and started eating as fast as they could. When the first pie was consumed, the second one was placed in front of the person. After several rounds of pies, a man and his son won after eating seven pies. They were paid fifty cents each for winning.

It had been a great day but by the end, everyone was tired and ready to go home.

Bill told everyone in his family, "Let's go get in the carriage and ride home; It is getting late."

The horses and carriages were brought around to them by the stable boys. Everyone was ready to go home. On the way home, Pam, Judy, June, and Jean had a great time talking about everything they did that day.

June told everyone, "We are going to have to start buying baby clothes for our little one."

Judy told them the baby was due in October and told everyone what she would need when it arrived.

Bill told Judy, "I will have a baby bed made."

Everyone was still talking when the carriage pulled up to the front

steps; Bill and John helped the ladies down and into the house. The men unloaded the wagon and took the horses to the barn and the wagon to the stall.

CHAPTER TEN

AUNT PENNY'S VISIT

One lovely cool spring morning, Joe's aunt came to visit. The carriage pulled up in front of the house as Jane sat gently rocking back and forth in the front yard swing with a shawl around her shoulders. Joe heard the carriage and came out the front door to meet his aunt. Joe helped his Aunt Penny step down.

After hugging his Aunt Penny Joe noticed a slight, young Negro girl coming out of the carriage behind her. Her mistress immediately piled bags into her arms. The girl stumbled backward and dropped one of the four bags on the ground.

Joe told Jim, 'Handle the bags for her."

Penny told Joe, "She's been useless since we left the steamship, throwing up, stumbling around like a drunken sot. How embarrassing. You'd think niggers would be used to ships by now. After all, they sail clear across the other side of the earth. You'd think riding a ship would be second nature to them."

Joe's Aunt Penny had long, beautiful chestnut hair knotted in a bun complemented by pretty blue eyes and a perfect nose; but she was fat, and getting fatter. She had come to stay for two weeks with Joe while Pam was in Vicksburg. She was there to help him run the plantation, but two days later all she had done was eat and lay in bed.

The next evening, Dora and Joan assisted with Aunt Penny's welcome dinner party. Joe had invited Pam's family and their friends to dinner so that they could meet his aunt.

67

Jane was cooking as fast as she could go. She told Dora, "If you don't hurry up with the napkins, I'm going to whip you."

As Joan sat peeling a mountain of potatoes, Aunt Penny walked into the kitchen. She walked over and lifted the lids of the pots to see what was smelling so good. Jane smiled at her and told her, "We will be serving everything in a few minutes."

Before walking back out to the dining room Aunt Penny told her to hurry up; she was starving.

Dora rolled her eyes at Joan and said, "Can you believe her?"

A few minutes later, the guests started to arrive. Joe spoke to them all as he welcomed them and introduced them to his aunt. Aunt Penny was nice to them but couldn't wait to eat. Everyone was seated, and Jane and the girls started serving food.

"Yes, ma'am, I am going to get you a nice clean fork right away. I will be right back." Dora burst through the kitchen door. Her wide smile quickly turned to a frown. "Lord knows, I have a notion to put that bowl of gravy all over that woman and leave it sitting right there on top of her head. If that old woman wasn't so busy shoveling food down her throat so fast, she would still have a fork to eat with. She is about to run me crazy. Give me a fork Joan."

"Lord help you," Joan laughed, reaching into the sink and giving Dora three forks. She quickly washed and dried them with her dishrag.

Dora said," She hasn't even started on dessert yet."

Dora's mama, Jane, told her, "You better mind your manners, child, before Master Joe hears you talking about his aunt like that." Jane was at the stove tending to a sea of steaming pots and pans, cooking more food for Joe's guest. "Master Joe is counting on you to be nice and help serve his aunt any way you can. "

"Yes, ma'am, but I don't have any legs left. If she doesn't quit eating, she is going to be as big as a cow." Dora headed back toward the dining room with a big smile on her face.

As Jane looked up at the ceiling, she shook her head. "What are we going to do with that child?" she asked Joan before returning to her cooking.

Everyone was having a great time at the little dinner party. They all told Joe that they enjoyed both the food and the company.

Joan was the plantation washwoman handling mountains of laundry on wash days. On days when there was no laundry to be done or during lavish dinner parties or holiday feasts, she and Dora would assist in the kitchen, helping cook and clean the plantation. Joan would also help serve; Dora was limited to the kitchen while Aunt Penny was at the plantation. She couldn't wait until Aunt Penny left; she was ready to start crawling on the floor from exhaustion.

Joan also worked in the fields when Master Joe needed her to pick cotton and chop grass away from the corn. Even though Joan was small she was a particularly good worker. She couldn't talk when she arrived but after her lessons with Dora, she was now able to speak remarkably well.

Joe had liked her from the start. Master Joe had gone to town by the river to buy slaves, and he bought Joan from a slave trader two years earlier. She wasn't but eleven years old at the time. Joe had bought two more slaves at the same time and loaded them into his wagon. He had a cot on the back porch and told Joan to sleep there until the men slaves could build a one-room cabin.

When Joe had Jim and some of the other slaves build the new house for when he and Pam got married, he also had them build an immense washhouse. It was complete with a water pump, washtubs, and a hearth for heating flat irons which sat on a table to the side along with two more rows of row houses. A coach house was built to provide storage for the wagons and carriages. Adjoining the stables were endless chicken coops where Jane would have plenty of eggs to cook with. There were several tool sheds built, and barns to fill with livestock. There was a large white fence around the backyard so the horses could roam freely in the huge pastures by day.

Joe was a handsome man in his early thirties with a luxurious head of black hair, sparkling blue eyes, and a vibrant smile; these were just some of the reasons Pam fell in love with him. Pam was much loved by Joe's slaves; she was found to be fair and talked generously to everyone. Pam would quickly become a beloved mistress when she and Joe married. She was soft-spoken and gentle, always had a wide, imperfect young person's smile on her face, and always had a kind word to say to Joe's servants. Joe was always cleanshaven; only Pam ever saw him otherwise. Joe was always blessed with wealth, and without question, the most handsome man Pam had ever met.

Dora came into Joe's library to bring him coffee, and he was sitting there in deep thought. He was missing Pam and wanted her to hurry home. Just as Joe took his first sip of coffee Jim ran in and told Master Joe a big storm was coming out of the south. Joe jumped up, set his coffee cup down, and rolled up his sleeves as he started toward the door and started helping the servants board up windows and clear out fallen trees and debris. He always pitched in for tasks that should be reserved for his slaves, but Joe wasn't that way. He worked right alongside them. The wind was blowing seventy miles an hour, the fence was blown down, and the horses were getting out.

Joe hollered for Jim to get some of the male slaves to help him catch the horses and put them in the barn. Jim jumped on Joe's horse Star with his rope and started roping as many horses as he could. The slaves put all the horses in the barn, but the toolsheds went down with the wind. Debris and trees were everywhere, and it looked like it was going to take every slave Joe had to clean the land up. For two days, Joe and his slaves worked hard, but, finally, the yard was looking better. Joe and his slaves were given out, but everyone had worked hard and done a great job.

"There is only a little damage to the roof, but it won't take long to fix it," Joe said. "I am going to have a party for all of you," he told Jim. Jim couldn't wait to tell Jane and the others.

Tables were brought out; the ladies made enough food to feed everyone, and everyone got their music items and sat and played around the open fire. Everyone was eating and sitting around the fire singing. They broke into merriment and songs, invoking giddiness and laughter from all around them. For no apparent reason, Joe and Jim kicked up their heels to lively fiddles, spoon playing, and washboard tunes; everyone enjoyed the big festive celebration.

Finally, around ten, everyone started cleaning up everything. They had to get some sleep to work the next morning at six. The next morning, the field hands woke up bright and early. Joe dressed his field hands better than average; he bought every one of them new clothes. Everyone was always working and building. The cabin row consisted of endless rows of neat, solidly built brick duplex slave quarters, like a tiny village. They each had a full-size bed, dresser, and a small table. The ladies planted a few flowers by their door.

Joan and Dora took a break and walked down by the river and sat down on a log. Flowers were growing beautifully all up and down the river. As Joan watched the moving water, she couldn't help but wonder what lay beyond the river. She would often stop her chores and stare out of the small window of the washroom with clothes piled up all around her. Dora would always smile at her when she saw her doing this.

"What are you thinking, Joan?" Dora asked her one day.

"I am watching how free the squirrels are and sometimes wish it was me."

"What do you think it is like out there, Joan?" Dora asked.

"As free as those squirrels running around in those trees, not a care in the world, Dora. I want to be just like the white people, not a care in the world with someone waiting on me. You know what I mean, Dora?"

"I do," said Dora.

Joan said, "I used to go into town with Master Joe, We would go to the general store, and he would tie the horses to the pole. Master Joe would talk to me, and we had a great time riding into town. He would buy me a stick of candy, but it has been so long, I done forgot what it looks like out there."

"It is about the same. When I was with Mama, the last time Master Joe and her went I saw white ladies walking down the sidewalks with fancy dresses on and beautiful hats on their heads. Some of them had a man to walk with them. The women would have their hand on their man's arm and when they looked at each other you could see how much in love they were. You ain't lived till you seen such as that," she snickered. Then she told Joan, "We better get back to work. This pile of clothes is not going to wash itself."

Joan looked out the window again and told Dora, "One of these days, I am going to ride me a big fancy horse right down that drive, clean to the promised land."

Dora told her, "And I will go with you hand in hand."

CHAPTER ELEVEN

JOAN BY THE RIVER

Joan sat by the river picking flowers. She was seventeen and didn't have a boyfriend, and it was beginning to look like she would be an old maid. Joan couldn't find any man she wanted as a husband despite her best efforts. Every day she went down to the river and watched the steamboats go by with men working on the decks. She wanted to be free so badly, and Dora told her she would go with her.

But would she go when the time came? She battled the memories of Ben Allen and a few more suitors that turned out to be worthless. If she could get to New York, the promised land, she would be free. She knew it would take a lot of planning, and she would have to leave her Master Joe, but she wanted to go so badly and see what free land was like. Like the youngest slave ladies her age, she desperately wanted a good husband and a nice home. But what man would be suitable for a mixed-breed plantation slave? She watched the steamboats and swans for a few more minutes before she got up with her basket of flowers. She went to Jane's kitchen and arranged the flowers nicely in a vase to put on Master Joe's dining room table, but her mind was still on the promised land AND a good husband.

Joan spent the better part of the morning cleaning the kitchen for Jane after breakfast. That morning, Joe's aunt went home, "Praise the Lord," and left a big mess all over the house. After pulling off all the sheets from the beds, Joan went off to the washroom to do laundry. Dora had to work in the kitchen helping Jane and couldn't help Joan. Joan missed talking to her as she worked. She looked out the window and saw a man sitting by the rocks as she washed the clothes. A handsome man she had never seen before. He appeared to be relaxing, trying to catch a breeze after working in the yard. She had no idea who he was, but she wanted to know him badly. He looked over and saw her by the window, and she turned away, too shy to come out.

The young man got up, walked over to the washroom, and said, "Hey, what are you doing?" Joan looked down as she was too shy to look up at him, but he just stood there, which forced her to look up. He was as tall as the oak tree by the washroom. He didn't have his shirt on, and his arms looked as if they were carved out of stone. He picked his shirt off the log he had been sitting on and slowly put it back on as he watched her.

"I am trying to catch a breeze; from working out here, it is warm heat today," he said as Joan slowly took in his features. His skin was a dark tan, his hair a beautiful mass of silky black waves. He had the prettiest brown eyes she had ever seen, and when he smiled, he showed her the most dazzling white teeth. He was handsome; he took good looks to a whole new level. He reached out his hand to her. "I'm Jacob Jeans." He smiled. Joan stared at him, not responding as he looked down at her with those beautiful eyes, "What's your name?"

Joan looked up at him and told him in a shy voice, "My name is Joan."

"Nice to meet you, Miss Joan. Why don't we have a seat by the river? I ain't going to bite you. I promise I will walk you back." Joan walked over to the seat by the river and sat down next to him.

"You come from the auction house?" Joan asked him.

"No. I grew up here. I have been going up north for a while working. Now I'm back." He told Joan. "I have been all over Mississippi, Arkansas, Louisiana; all over the south, Canada, and New York. I have been working on the steamboat and doing work for Joe. Joe owns the Dixie Bell Streamline that carries cotton to other states. I have been going up and down the river working on the deck unloading for him."

As Joan looked at the river, she told him, "What I wouldn't give to go to the promised land." She laughed as they talked. "You a part of the house staff?" she asked him.

He told her, "Yes, I am here to stay." She was so glad; she liked the way he looked and talked.

Joan told Jacob how Master Joe bought her and brought her home to work for him in the fields. Joan couldn't talk when she first came to Master Joe's plantation, but she learned a few words after Dora's lessons and working in the field with others. She told him she slept on a cot on the back porch before Master Joe had Jim and others build her a room on the row.

Joan barely remembered the auction block. But she did remember the stench of unwashed bodies, acrid fear, and overwhelming grief that permeated the air. It wasn't good. Joan would have sworn that she tasted the acid on her tongue for months afterward. She told him that her mama was sold to someone else and that they had been put in a shed the first day.

She and her mama were inspected like cattle. Some men pulled open their mouths to look at their teeth and pinched their arms to see if they were weak, but most seemed to tell on sight that she and her mama were as healthy as could be.

They poked and prodded Joan as her mama was taken away. She always wondered why they had taken her mama and didn't take her too. Joan remembered being enraged, fighting the men taking her mama as they threw her to the ground. Joan lay on the ground crying with her arms and hands in the air reaching for her mama. Joan knew she would never see her mama again as the buyer dragged her mama away in the wagon and chained her to the bars.

She felt like grabbing a board and hitting anything within her reach as the trader dragged her back to the auction block. Instead, she pushed her anger down deep and tried to ignore what was happening around her. She was so lonely and afraid. She didn't know what was going to happen to her. After Master Jenkins bought her and brought her to his home, she had nightmares. Joan's smile went away.

He cocked his head sideways and told her, "That is a shame." He asked her, "How long have you been here Joan?"

She told him, "Six years."

He began to nod. "I remember you. You were just eleven when Joe bought you. You used to run around in the fields giving Ben and Jerry a fit while they taught you how to hoe cotton. You would cry and stomp the cotton. You would try to tell everyone you didn't want to work, but you could only say a few words. But they got the message."

Jacob stood up and reached for Joan's hand. As they walked hand in hand up the hill, Jacob knew she was the one for him and bent over and placed a kiss on her lips. It was the first time Joan had been kissed. Jacob pulled his lips back and smiled at her.

Joan lay on her cot that night and stared at the ceiling. She dreamt of being Jacob's wife and going to New York. Putting her fingers to her lips, she remembered the kiss he gave her. She hugged her pillow until she fell asleep. The next morning Joan took a bath around the back of her cabin row and put on her best dress. Pam had given it to her out of her trunk. Joan put a ribbon in her hair right before leaving to work in the kitchen with Jane and Dora.

As she walked in the back door, Mrs. Jane said, "Well, look at you all dolled up. Who is the fellow?" Joan just smiled and started washing dishes and singing to herself.

Jacob came by the washroom. "I need to talk to you. Master Jenkins told me this morning that I am going back on the steamship." Jacob and Joan both hated it, but they knew that was the way it would always be. Jacob left the next morning, and they never saw each other again. Her heart broke as she watched him leave on a steamboat going down the river. He waved at her until the boat went around the bend.

CHAPTER TWELVE

PAM IS ON HER WAY HOM

Pam had a great time with her cousins, but she had a wedding to get ready for. Pam sent a letter to Joe asking him to pick her up at the stagecoach Saturday morning.

My dearest Joe, a year ago tonight, you first told me you loved me and asked me to be your wife. You changed my life that evening and put us on a path that brings us such joy. When I look at you, I realize my love for you grows deeper, richer, and more satisfying as time goes by. You're the first person I want to tell whenever something good happens. When something bad happens, I know that I can count on you to take me in your arms and tell me everything will be alright.

I'm the luckiest woman in the world because I can honestly say that I'm in love with my best friend. There is not another man in the world that can hold a candle to you, my darling, and I just want to let you know that I love you more than even the most heartfelt words can express.

Being apart from you has been more difficult than I ever imagined. I see reminders of you everywhere I look, and they make me ache to be near you again. Tonight, as I write this letter, it feels like you are right here with me. I feel your hand on my waist, your fingers in my hair, and the soft breath of your kiss on my cheek. I will be arriving on the stagecoach Saturday at one.

Love Pam

As soon as Pam returned home, she and May were to meet five of Pam's bridesmaids back at Betty's for dress fittings. Betty had a lot of Pam's dress done, and Pam fell in love with it. It was exactly like she wanted it.

Betty measured the other girls and told them, "Come back Friday to make sure your dresses fit properly." Everyone loved Betty and hugged her bye.

Betty was a sweet woman and had been making dresses for twenty-five years. Pam's wedding was one of the biggest dress orders she had ever done, and she only had one hundred and fifteen days to finish them. She needed to work day and night to complete them on time. Betty had a small one-room shop. An old wooden table for her sewing machine and cut fabric took up most of the room.

Betty made sure she sat where she had a view of the front door to ensure she would see any customer that came in. She didn't want to miss them. Betty often would sew for sixteen hours a day; a candle stood in front of her casting a glow over the room. She was busy working on Pam's dress when she heard a cough. She looked up to see a lady that needed a dress hemmed. The lady required the dress for the next day and told Betty she would wait. Betty leaned forward, took the dress from the lady, and made stitches around the bottom of the dress. She handed it back to the lady and told her that it would be fifty cents.

Betty went back to making Pam's wedding dress with layers and layers of fabric. She didn't even hesitate when the needle slipped, stabbing the meaty center of her finger.

Betty never married and felt like sometimes her whole life had been about attaching one piece of fabric to another. She made many wedding dresses but never one for herself.

Betty's dreams were of another lady's wedding. She gave up on herself a long time ago. Now she was doing Miss Pam's wedding dress. Betty moved the candle closer to see better as she sewed the train. She knew she needed to hurry if she was going to finish Pam's dress before going to the back to eat.

Betty had two little nieces, and Christmas was coming soon. Even though the fabric was cheap and would last until the following Christmas, she always made new clothes for her sister and the girls. Their clothes were nothing like the silk and lace that Betty's fingers danced across day in and day out at her shop. It was sturdy and long-lasting, and that was all that mattered. Betty could only see them every two months because of all her work. She didn't have much time for doing anything other than sewing, eating, and sleeping.

When Pam came into Betty's shop Friday morning, her mouth dropped open. Her finished wedding dress was hanging across the room. Betty needed to have Pam try it on and see if anything needed fixing. She had to put a few stitches in the waist, and it was ready for Pam to take home. Pam was so excited as she stepped up into the carriage with her wedding dress over her arm; she couldn't wait to get home and try it on again.

Jim shut the door for her and climbed up in the top seat. It began to rain, and he pulled his hat down over his ears. He had no way to keep from getting wet. He told Star, the horse, "Just get us home."

The rain started coming down harder, and Star was having a hard time in the mud. It was a lousy ride, and Pam had difficulty holding on. It was five miles on the muddy road, but Jim and Star made it to the plantation and pulled up in front. Jim jumped down as Joe came out with an umbrella and opened the door to the carriage for Pam. He took her dress and helped her down, and they both ran into the house laughing.

Once they got into the house, Joe grabbed a towel and dried Pam off. He then took her It was bad luck. She ran up the stairs with the dress over her arm.

in his arms and kissed her. He wanted to see her wedding dress, but she told him

Dora ran up the stairs right behind her with towels. She had prepared a hot bath for Pam so she would not get chilled and get sick. Pam told Dora to help her out of her wet clothes. Dora went to the chifforobe and laid out

Pam's clothes across the bed. Pam had laid her wedding dress down, and Dora hung it up to dry it from the rain.

Pam stepped into the bath, and Dora poured more hot water in. As Pam lay in the warm water, she dreamt of her wedding. Pam stepped out of the tub, and Dora put a towel around her shoulders and dried her back off. Pam had her hair up in a towel, and as she pulled the towel off, her long hair dropped to her waist. Dora helped her get dressed and brushed her hair out into long beautiful waves. Dora fixed Pam's hair up into a knot on the back of her neck and put a feather in her hair.

Pam looked gorgeous. Jane knocked on the door and informed her that Joe was ready and waiting for her downstairs. Pam had wanted to try on her wedding dress but knew she didn't have time. Joe was taking her out for supper to celebrate their engagement. She glanced back at her dress one more time before heading downstairs with a smile.

They were going to town for dinner at the Beechwood Restaurant for a fine dinner for just the two of them. Joe wanted to celebrate their engagement with steaks and seafood. The restaurant was friendly, with a beautiful dining room. It had a full bar for a nice dinner drink and a dance floor.

Jim brought the carriage around as Joe and Pam walked out the front door hand-in-hand. Jim stepped down off the top seat and opened the door for them. Joe helped Pam up the step and inside. It had stopped raining and had turned into a beautiful day. Joe opened the window for fresh air as they rode the five miles to town.

Jim pulled up in front of the Beechwood Restaurant, and Joe stepped out of the carriage and helped Pam down with his hands around her waist. As she stepped onto the street, Joe took her hand, and they walked inside together.

The hostess seated them in a cozy corner with a candle on the table and asked them, "Will you like some wine before dinner?"

Joe took the wine menu and ordered. "Two white wines," and then "two middle steak dinners."

The couple enjoyed the terrific dinner. The staff was very friendly and made sure they were ready to wait on them at a moment's notice.

"We will have to come back again sometime. The steaks were excellent." Joe told the waiter.

It was getting dark as Joe and Pam rode back home. It was a romantic night by the lake, with the steady clip-clop of horse's hooves and the sweet things Joe was whispering in Pam's ear. They wanted to take this wonderful romantic feeling with them as they stepped off the carriage by the lake. With all the planning of the wedding, Joe wanted a few minutes alone with Pam. It was relaxing and peaceful in the countryside. Joe had told Pam, about this spot but wasn't able to do it justice. They had a beautiful view of downtown. Joe put his arm around her waist and pulled her tenderly to him as the sat down on a log.

Joe told Pam that she was the most beautiful woman he had ever seen as he kissed her madly on the lips.

As Joe kissed her one more time before they got back into the carriage, he told her, "Our honeymoon is a time to indulge, celebrate, and create new memories.

CHAPTER THIRTEEN

GETTING READY FOR THE WEDDING

Bride-to-be Pam had been a busy bee. She and Joe had walked through every step of the ceremony, including their vows, during the last-minute practice run. They knew the church was going to be full of many, many people, a lot of whom they'd never met, and they just wanted to think about themselves and what it meant to them.

Pam, June, and May had everything ready. Pam tried on her wedding dress and showed it to her mother, June, and her friend, May. It was lovely and fit her perfectly. The invitations had been mailed, and four hundred guests were coming. Jane was making a five-layer cake. Pam and Joe had gone over how they wanted Jane to set up the wedding breakfast table in true royal style.

Joe told Jim to make sure the tables were set correctly in the perfect way to bring a bit of high society glamour to the reception. Jim and some of the slave men brought in enough tables and set them up in the dining room for eight guests at each table.

Jane had Dora and Joan do a formal place setting. "If you want to follow the royals, then nothing says special occasion more than a classic white tablecloth. However, if you want an instant update to this traditional look, but one that still retains a sophisticated elegance, then go dark. Dark charcoal or navy cloth will create a very contemporary feel, the setting against white or ornate crockery and silver or gold cutlery. Napkins should be simply folded - no swans, please!" The girls giggled. "Place them either in the center of the place setting or to the left on their side plate." As the girls set the tables following Jane's instructions, Jane stood in the corner watching to make sure they got everything right.

As the kitchen slaves came into the dining room, Jane told them, "First, make sure everyone has as much room as possible and that every place in the setting is evenly spaced out. Next, the dinner plate should always be at the center of your setting and directly in front of your guest. Set each side plate to the left of the main dinner plates and be sure they are evenly set - if they are not used. Place knives and spoons to the right of the dinner plate and forks to the left. The blade edge of the knife is always facing inward towards your plate."

"The key is to work from the outside in towards the center, with the cutlery for the first course on the outermost. So, if you're starting with soup, this will be your soup spoon. For a salad starter, then this will be your salad knife on the right and the salad fork on the left. If you have bread, then a small butter knife is placed on or near the side plate. Cutlery for the dessert course is set at the top of the place setting with the fork prongs facing towards the right and the spoon bowl towards the left so you will naturally pick up the spoon with your right hand and the fork with your left. The spoon will also sit above the fork. Place all the glassware above and to the right of the dinner plate and include a glass of water, red wine, or white wine. If appropriate for the occasion," she told them, "As will most likely be the case for a wedding breakfast, include a champagne flute as well."

"Once you have your table organized, you can then add your finishing touches like flowers." Jane showed them, "Once you master the layout for your tables, you can get creative and have some fun dressing and accessorizing your tables for the big day. Ideas and styles are limitless just have a flick through magazines for more inspiration."

"But to create a royal feel for your tables, I suggest, girls can't go too far wrong with a large floral centerpiece or candelabra, making sure the flowers are where the guests can see over them to talk," she said, as she walked around the tables looking at their work.

Jane had them change a few things, but everything was looking great. Jane told them, "Joe and Pam are having the centerpieces made for the tables and they will be here the night before the wedding breakfast. Jane told the girls," Come to the kitchen. We have a lot of cooking to do for four hundred guests". Jane sat down and made out a list for the royal dinner so she could go to the grocery store ahead of time and have everything ready to cook.

Pam wanted Jane to do a buffet along the wall. "For breakfast, we will have eggs, sausage, bacon, gravy, biscuits, and fruit," Pam told Jane as they walked along the buffet. Everyone can walk by the buffet and fill their plates. We will set the coffee pot at the end with the china cups and spoons along with a pitcher of orange juice. Ensure you have plenty of ice in the water glasses right before the guests come into the room. "

Jane told Jim she needed to go to the store for all the food for breakfast and the wedding dinner. Jane knew there would be twenty people in the wedding party and they would be eating breakfast at nine in the morning before the wedding the next day.

Jane had Dora and Joan cleaning the plantation home for the guests who would be spending the night but told them to hurry so they could help her in the kitchen. All the meats were in the ovens when she sat down for a minute to rest before making the yeast rolls and covering them with a towel to allow them to rise. Dora and Joan came running into the kitchen, giggling and laughing.

"We do not have time for foolishness. We have to work," Jane told them as she handed them aprons to put around their waists. "Start on the pots and pans."

Joan and Dora looked at each other and rolled their eyes, smiling on the way to the sink.

Jane woke up at 3:00 am the next morning and rolled over to wake up Jim. Both of them had a lot of work to do. Jane walked into the kitchen at four and saw that Joan and Dora were already there getting pans out for breakfast. Joan was getting out the bacon and sausage and putting it all in two pans. Dora was cracking eggs for the wedding breakfast. Jane pulled out the fruit and put on the coffee. Then Jane squeezed out the oranges and made two pitchers of juice. They set the tables yesterday, and by 8:50, everything was on the buffet for the wedding guests. Jane was worn out, but she didn't have time to sit down.

Pam was up getting ready, and Joe was in his bedroom. At 8:30, they came down to check everything out. The first guest arrived at 8:55, and Jim opened the door, as Pam and Joe came out of the dining room hall. It was Mr. and Mrs. Jacob Steven; they were the best man, and one of the bridesmaids. Just a few minutes later four more carriages pulled up. Jim greeted them all and showed them inside.

Everyone headed for the wedding breakfast room and was shaking hands with everyone and ready to eat. Joe and Pam were so happy and enjoying everyone at the tables. Jane, Joan, and Dora did a great job, and everyone enjoyed the food and talk about what they were going to do at the wedding.

After breakfast, everyone went to the ballroom to practice a couple of times. The wedding would be the next day at two. Pam led the ladies upstairs to try on their dresses and let them take them home.

After everyone left, Jane told Joan and Dora, "Clean the tables off and get them set up for tomorrow."

Joan took the tablecloths out to wash and iron so they could be cleaned and pressed to be put back on all the tables for the wedding dinner the next day. Jane and Dora washed all the dishes and cleaned up the kitchen and started the wedding dinner. By the next morning, everything was ready for dinner at four. Joan and Dora set the buffet up again with all the food.

Jane was ready to get into bed. After Joan and Dora removed all the food, and dishes and cleaned up the kitchen, Jane went to her shack and fell into bed.

CHAPTER FOURTEEN

JANE GETS A SURPRISE

Jane and Jim got up for the day. Jane had the coffee going in Master Jenkin's kitchen and had just put the bacon on when someone knocked on the back door.

Jane went to the door, and a young white man asked, "Mrs. Jane?" The man had a southern accent and a nice-sounding voice.

"Yes," Jane said.

"I've been looking for you for a long time; you're not an easy woman to find. I was just told you, and your husband was sold to Master Jenkins a few years ago."

Jane saw the man had a large manilla envelope in his hand. She and Jim stood in the doorway looking at the man with their mouths hanging open.

"Forgive me," he said and started again. "My name is Jack Wells, and I am a lawyer from Vicksburg, Mississippi. I'm here to talk to you, Mrs. Jane, about your great uncle's estate."

Jane eased the door open but kept her hand on the doorknob. "What?" Jane asked as she looked at the man as if he was crazy.

The man started yet again, "I am Jack Wells. Your great uncle Joe Hack has died and left you, his estate."

Jim told the man to come inside so that Jane could sit down at the table.

"You must be mistaken," she told him. "I know you have ridden a long way to find me, but I can't believe anyone would leave me anything."

Mr. Wells told her, "No, no, I am quite certain. I have been searching for you through the slave trader's records for a long time. Just recently I found someone who had your sell records and they told me where you were."

Jane finally had her voice back and told Mr. Wells, "Maybe we need to talk about this over some coffee and this food on the stove. We can eat while you tell us about whatever you have in that folder you are holding." Jane took a rag and wiped a chair off and asked him to sit down.

The man sat down without hesitation letting the bulk of his case rest on the chair beside him. Jane eyed the dirty dishes in the sink, hoping he didn't notice all the flour that she had gotten on the floor making biscuits that morning. The man continued pulling papers out of his folder.

As Mr. Wells shuffled the papers around looking as if he was searching for something important, Jane had a moment to collect her thoughts. Her father died when she was nine, and her mother lived in Vicksburg, Mississippi. She knew her grandfather grew up in the system. Her grandmother never knew where her husband went after Jane was born, and her grandmother died of cancer when her momma was twenty-one. She knew she had no relatives but her mother. She was sure because surely one of her three social workers would have diligently looked for some relative before dumping her into Mississippi Child Services.

"Mr. Wells," Jane said.

"Call me Jack," he replied.

"Mr. Wells. I'm afraid I don't understand. What estate?"

Jack Wells opened the envelope and pulled out a large color photograph. "This one."

His fingers pushed the image toward her. A house? No, not a house. More like a mansion. One of the old Southern mansions with white column poles and everything. Jane thought she was going to pass out. She looked back up at Mr. Wells, not quite sure what to make of it. "You're joking, right?"

He looked confused, then took her hand and said, "No, ma'am. It is the home of Mr. Joe Hawk, your great uncle." His voice softened slightly when he spoke his name but then quickly returned to its smooth, businesslike Southern drawl.

Jane couldn't believe it. "No, I don't have any relatives."

Mr. Wells raised his eyebrow. "Mr. Hawk was your father's brother. He told me so himself when he made some adjustments to his will two months before he died."

Jane looked at him again, her forehead wrinkled as she sorted out the implications of Mr. Wells' simple statement. "But my father said he grew up in the system. He 'doesn't have a family."

Mr. Wells nodded slowly and looked at her for what seemed like an exceptionally long moment. "Your father's mother, Joe's baby sister, dabbled in some, well, not genuinely nice things. She brought home boyfriends who are less than reputable. One night, probably after having a beating again, your father ran away. He was sixteen. Your mother reported him missing, but they never heard from him again for years."

Jane studied a board on the wall. "If that's so, how'd you find me, and how are you even sure you have the right woman?"

"Joe Hawk never gave up looking for you. The day he came to me to change his will, he finally had a lead on you. He had also gotten a lead on your father," Mr. Wells said. "He went north and changed his name, taking on the last name of some farmer or something."

Jane had a small smile tug at the corner of her mouth just thinking about someone who wanted her.

"Anyway," Wells continued, " He says he found out your father married his sister and had a child, a girl, but your father had come back to see your mother, and they died in a car crash. He didn't know your name. He only knew that their daughter would have been roughly nine years old when her parents died."

Jane looked at Mr. Well's big eyes but declined to speak. She thought he seemed sincere, and all his information checked out. Still, it was a lot for Jane to accept just yet. Jane knew the woman she called mama was a foster mama to her. Jane told him to continue.

Mr. Wells cleared his throat and leaned into the seat of the chair. "Since he had no children of his own, and Sue was his only sister the girl would be his only heir."

"He asked me to start looking before he died, so I did. But it took a long time, and the good Lord took him home just a few days before I found your records." He paused and leaned forward before saying, "Joe left everything he owned to you."

Jane looked up at him and said, "Everything?"

Mr. Wells nodded his nice clean-shaven face and told her, "Yes. The house and all its contents, and the remaining balance in his checking account." He pulled a paper from the folder. "Which totals just over forty-five thousand dollars, as you see here."

Jane thought she was going to pass out; she couldn't believe this man. She tried to swallow but found her mouth severely lacking the necessary moisture to do so. "Forty-five thousand dollars and you're sure it's me?"

Mr. Wells grinned, revealing even white teeth. He told Jane, "I'll just need you to sign a few papers, please."

He handed her his pen across the table, and she signed her name at the bottom of the last page. She still couldn't believe it as she told Mr. Wells, "bye' and closed the door. She promised him that she would look over all the papers and meet up with him to see her new home in a few days.

"It looks like we are going to be traveling deeper south than we intended to, but Master Jenkins has to okay it and give me my freedom papers," Jane told Jim.

Jim and Jane watched Mr. Wells ride his horse down the long drive. Jane gathered the papers from the folder and stepped into the bright June sunshine outside so that she could read every word. Jane sat down in her old rocking chair as thick warm air settled around her, and she inhaled a deep breath of the air.

"I think I am going to cry," she said to Jim.

She listened to the birds' twitter before looking at the documents again. Jane pulled out the photograph again and looked at the house that would be hers and her family's. It was beautiful. Jim and Jane studied every inch of it more closely. Chipping paint hung in flakes in several spots, and one of the front shutters sagged.

"It doesn't matter; I will fix it like new," Jim said.

A small seed of hope sprouted in Jane's mind. Maybe, for once, something good was about to happen in her life. Joe Hack had left everything to his sister's daughter. There was a picture of her grand uncle and grand aunt in the folder; she looked at them for a long time and then started crying. Someone loved her after all.

As she looked at the papers she noticed a newspaper article. She picked it up and began to read. "Crash kills Three, Wounds Two. A drunk driver took an exit ramp onto Interstate 57 last night around 8:00 PM, meeting one car head-on and causing two others to crash. Paul Hawks, 32, a factory worker, and his wife Sue, 31, a teacher, were both killed instantly in the head-on collision. Joan Wheeler, 50, rear-ended the Hawks' car. The Hawks were taken by ambulance but died before arriving at the hospital. Authorities say the drunk driver and her passenger both sustained significant injuries, but they are expected to recover. Their identities have not yet been released. The police say the driver will be facing DUI charges and possibly..." Jane didn't want to read any more and already knew how the story ended. Jane thought to herself, the paper knows the facts but doesn't know everything.

Only Jane knew her daddy wanted to come back to his family; how her daddy saved for months to come back home to them. Jane hadn't been in the car. Her dad and mom went to a fancy restaurant in the city for the evening to talk about things. She remembered how pretty her mama Sue looked in her red dress as they walked out the front door of their friend Carol's home. They kissed Jane bye right before they left for the evening and told her they would be back soon.

Jane placed the paper down. Now she knew her last name before she married Jim. It represented the first dark cloud in a series of thunderstorms in her life. As Jane sat there in her rocker, she said, "Enough of the past." The wind started blowing and she went inside.

Jane knew she needed to start Master Jenkin's dinner. She knew she needed to figure out her next steps for the future. As she tapped her fingers on the armrest, she knew she needed some guidance, some advice. She would have to ask the lawyer, Mr. Wells, the next time she went to Vicksburg.

On Monday, the next week, Jane and Jim traveled to Vicksburg to the lawyer's office to sort through everything. As they rode up in the wagon, Jane looked for Mr. Wells' office on Court Street. Jim pulled up in front of the lawyer's office and tied the reins to the pole.

As they went inside, Mr. Wells got up from his desk, shook Jim's hand, and told them, "Come on in and sit down, and let's go over the folder," he said. "First, we need to go over to the bank and cash the bank accounts." He asked, "Do you want to put the house up for sale or move into it?"

Jane told him she wanted to think about it, she was not a free slave, and she would have to buy their freedom from Master Jenkins.

Jane knew that if she sold the house, she could live a happy life with that kind of money. Maybe she and Jim could retire and buy a small home with Dora going to a good school. All Jane knew today was that she could launch a new future. Jane knew she had a lot to think about.

"With us being slaves, what do we have to do to get our freedom papers?" Jane asked Mr. Wells.

"I have written a letter to Mr. Jenkins telling him about your estate and asking him to release you and your family," he replied.

Mr. Wells had Jane and Jim sit down in front of the dark, carved wood desk. From the looks of his office, small-town law was going well.

"Jane, I'm so glad you came to my office." Jane looked up and saw Mr. Wells smiling at her. He rested his hand on her shoulder. "Now don't you worry about a thing; I will have this all covered. The law requires that we post an estate for ninety days in the paper before we can close."

He walked behind his desk and sat down in a large leather chair in front of where Jane sat poised on the edge of her seat.

"Ninety days?"

"But, since it took me a while to find you, there are just a few days, maybe a week left to go."

"Why do you have to post it for that long, "Jane asked. "I don't understand. Can someone else claim everything?"

"No, dear, it's not that," he said as he chuckled.

"Though Master Jenkins might wish it so. We must post it so that anyone has a debt to claim against the estate. They have the opportunity to collect from the holdings before the money is dispersed."

"Okay." Jane fought the urge to ask how many debts were coming out of the money.

"There are no outstanding debts save but the electricity bill, which I've already taken care of. It's just a formality," Mr. Wells told her.

He was looking at Jane as if he expected a reply from her, but she couldn't think of the proper one, so she said nothing.

"Well," Mr. Wells said, "Let's ride out there and give it a look, shall we?"

"Give what a look?" Jane asked after staring at him blankly for a moment.

"Why, the house, of course. I figure you'd want to see it, don't you?"

Jane looked up at him. "Oh, yes. Of course." She scooped up her old purse feeling rather stupid.

As they stepped out into the warm sunshine, Jack Wells got on his horse and rode in front of them. Jim and Jane followed in their wagon. They rode through the rest of town, which, as far as anyone could see, consisted of a hardware store, four more stores, and a tiny barbershop, and then they were out of town on a winding tree-lined road.

The sun was hot, and the air was blowing when they come upon a gravel road. As they rounded the treeline, Jane's jaw fell open so wide it nearly hit her lap. She couldn't believe it! The house was like nothing she had ever seen. Jane and Jim went up the front steps, and Mr. Wells opened the door. As Jane stood in the center of the grand entryway, she felt out of place. The cool metal of a borrowed key disappeared into the heat of her palm.

The mansion had huge stairs going up the middle of the home. Rooms everywhere. Jane knew she should be happy. Yet, she couldn't believe she deserved any of this. She had never even known this man. She hadn't gone to his funeral, and she didn't belong in this town. Jane shook her head and tried to force the voices out. Deserve or not, it was about to be hers. She surveyed her ancestral homestead. She felt slightly unnerved by the silence of all the rooms.

Everything was clean and tidy as if the owner stepped out for afternoon errands and didn't come back. Jane remembered being taken from her home and forced into the disgrace of being sold. Jane refused to let go of the faith in God that held her heart together. She was determined to survive in her new home; Jane never expected this.

The wide front door opened to a large entry and hall-type thing as Jane and Jim walked in. Flanking both sides were two massive oak and glass bookcases that reached nearly to the top of the sixteen-foot ceiling as Jane ran her hand along with the oak wood. Inside were various knickknacks and some books that looked to be at least a hundred years old. Not that Jane was an expert on such things. An open-door frame led into the dining room to her left, and to her right stood the parlor. A grand staircase rose to an overlook before twisting around into the upper levels. Looking up they marveled at the massive chandelier that sparkled with the afternoon light streaming through the window over the front door. Jane could see down the main hall through the floor-length windows on either side of the back door and onto the back porch from where she stood. The roof of what they assumed to be the old kitchen was just barely visible.

Mr. Wells had told her about the separate original plantation kitchen out back with the keeper quarters above, the potato and smokehouse, the barn, and the old slave cabins outback.

It was just too much to explore. Jane told Jim, "I got to sit down." Jim went and poured her a glass of water.

Ancient wooden floorboards squeaked underneath their feet as they made their way into the dining room. The room was bigger than any room they had ever been in. The room invited light with its floor-to-ceiling windows and lace curtains and ornate copper valances. A dozen dark wood and plush green velvet chairs flanked a carved wooden table that took up the center space. Jane resisted the urge to touch the delicate stacks of china in the display case as she passed into what was now the kitchen.

Mr. Wells said they had just put the kitchen inside the main house. "What could have been before that, she thought?"

There was an eating space for servants and storage for food. Jane thought she had died and gone to heaven in this new kitchen that was all hers. They crossed the main hall and entered Joe's bedroom, which was filled with his things. Brushes were still on top of a massive dressing table. A huge wooden bed sat in the middle of the room.

Jane opened what she thought was a closet door and saw stairs leading up. How weird. Jane's skin prickled as she peered up into the dim recess. They tried the first step of the very steep, very narrow stairway. Had they just discovered a secret passageway? At the top, she found herself in one of the four upper bedrooms. This wasn't at all what she expected.

Passing through the bedroom they entered another wide hallway on the second level, she eyed the staircase to the third floor. It led straight to a closed door. When she opened the door she found it led to a huge ballroom filled with old furniture. So much treasure, Jane couldn't wait to come back and look through all of it. Jane knew it was going to be there. She and Dora could go through it later.

Jane prayed all the way home that Master Jenkins would okay their freedom. As Jane looked up at the sky on the way home, a smile crossed her face. Only a few puffs of white clouds broke up the startling blue sky. Jane waved at a few people on the street as they rode along back to their cabin.

It was getting dark, and Jane still had to talk to Master Joe and cook dinner for him and Pam. Jane was praying God would have Master Joe give her their freedom papers. They had been working for him for a long time. Jane glanced back just as the mansion disappeared from view. She had gone to heaven and didn't even die.

As they rode up Master Joe's drive, Jane was still praying. Jim was going to talk to Master Joe about releasing them.

Jim knocked on Master Joe's door and was told to come in and have a seat. Jack Wells had given him a letter about Jane's estate, and he wanted Jim to have Master Joe sign the freedom papers and mail them back.

After the two men talked for a few minutes, Joe called Jane into the room with them. Once Jane was seated in front of the desk Joe told the couple that he was going to sign the freedom papers for them.

"Dora and Joan are getting freedom papers too."

Jane was so excited she had to stop herself from jumping out of the chair and hugging Master Jenkins. As she walked back to the kitchen she sang church songs, thanking God for being so good.

Jane still had Master Joe and Miss Pam's wedding dinner to do tonight. She cooked all the food in record time

CHAPTER FIFTEEN

WEDDING DAY

Pam woke up at 6 am. on the day of her wedding. Dora had her water ready for her bath. After Pam finished bathing Dora helped her dress and she left the guest room and went downstairs ready for breakfast. Joe was already there. Jane had made them bacon, eggs, gravy, and biscuits, with coffee.

Joe took Pam's hand and kissed it, and told her, "Tonight, you will be Mrs. Joe Jenkins."

Pam smiled at him and kissed him on the lips. After eating, Pam told him, "I have a lot to do today. My hairstylist will be here at twelve to do my hair, and then I am getting my makeup done at one."

"You look beautiful now," Joe said as he kissed her one last time before she left to get ready.

The hairdresser arrived at noon to work on Pam's hair. Pam's mother and her friend, May, helped her with her wedding dress. She had enough time to get her hair right and make any tweaks or changes. Her makeup stylists had her looking beautiful. All the bridesmaids had come at twelve to have three stylists work on their hair and makeup. There were six bridesmaids, and each person had thirty minutes with the stylist.

The stylist had told Pam, "When I arrive, I will start on your bridesmaids first. I prefer to have you go last so that when your photographer arrives, he will catch those last-minute "getting ready" shots with you looking fresh. Before applying your makeup I will prep your face.

This will give you time to relax and enjoy the day. We will have two hours before the wedding starts to do the final styling."

Pam had the photographer arrive two hours before she was ready to go down the stairs so he could get set up and take photos. She wanted him to take pictures of her while she was getting her makeup and hair styled.

The photographer told her that the extra time would allow him to take more flattering photos. He would be able to capture the details - gown, shoes, jewelry, etc. - in addition to the hustle and bustle of the room and the often emotional interactions between the bride and her bridesmaids and relatives.

After Pam was dressed in her gown, hair, and makeup, her mother put Pam's veil on top of her head and asked the stylist to make sure everything looked great.

Joe had his groomsmen arrive an hour and a half before the ceremony. When the music started Pam's bridesmaids lined up at the door so they would be ready to go down the stairs before the bride.

Guests were all seated in the ballroom. Pam's pastor was at the front, ready when the music started. All the guests stood up. When the music began, Joe and the groomsmen waited at the bottom of the stairs with Pam's dad. Pam's bridesmaids looked beautiful coming down the stairs. As each bridesmaid reached the bottom the groomsman took her arm and led her to the front of the ballroom.

The wedding march started and Pam walked out of her room to the top of the stairs where she stopped for a minute for her photo; everyone loved how she looked. Her dad went up the stairs, took Pam's arm, and slowly walked her down. Once they reached the bottom of the stairs Pam's dad kissed her on the cheek before giving her arm to Joe. The couple smiled at each other before Joe walked Pam down the aisle.

The pastor asked for everyone to take a seat; then started the ceremony.

Joe took Pam's hand and started his vows. "Pam, you are the first person I want to see in the morning and the last at night. I look forward to loving the smallest moments, like the way your eyes sparkle while you toss your hair back. Spin a coin into a fountain and make a wish for us. You are my wish come true. I vow to make my life forever yours and build my dreams around you. I take thee to be my wife, and I promise to look into your eyes just like I do now with love and soulful amazement. I can't wait to spend the rest of my life with you. I promise to be the man that you see now in your eyes, today, tomorrow, and always. I promise to be there to catch you if you should stumble, carry you over every threshold, and fall in love with you every day."

Pam looked into Joe's eyes lovingly. "Joe, I love you without fear, without hesitation, and promise to support you, encourage you, and cherish you as your wife. Live with me, laugh with me, love with me, in all things. I am so excited to be your wife and share the good times and learning experiences in every moment. I vow to take from every moment the opportunity to love and nurture you and I will be your devoted wife forevermore. You are my family, and I want to be there for you, grow with you, and never forget how lucky I am. Marriage is a verb. It is not something that happens in a moment but rather something that takes a lifetime. We pledge to marry for all time, to join our hearts on the journey of marriage. It is how we love every day. I take you as my husband and promise to be true to you."

Pastor Russell asked Joe and Pam, "Joe, will you have Pam to be your wife, to live together in holy marriage? Will you love her, comfort her, honor her, and keep her in sickness and in health, and forsaking all others, be faithful to her as long as you both shall live?"

Joe said, "Yes."

"Pam, will you have Joe to be your husband, to live together in holy marriage? Will you love him, comfort him, honor him, and keep him in sickness and in health, and forsaking all others, be faithful to him as long as you both shall live?"

Pam said, "Yes."

"In the name of God, I, Pastor Russell, take you, Joe and Pam, to be married and pronounce you husband and wife. Joe, you may kiss your bride."

After Joe and Pam went back down the aisle, the pastor told everyone to go to the dining room for the reception.

Joe, Pam, and their families sat at their table at the front of the room. They had decided to skip the receiving line and let the four hundred guests visit the couple's table during dinner. Joe and Pam had plans for everything from the wedding, to the photos, and their departure at eight.

Jane had everything looking lovely, and the food was ready. Jane had set up three buffet lines for the four hundred guests. Everyone went through fast and was having a great time eating and talking.

Ben gave a toast to Joe and Pam while men slaves brought around trays of cocktails. Ben's toast started with the bridesmaids and then the groomsmen. After two hours of dinner and congrats for the bride and groom, the bride and groom gave a toast to each other and their guests. The tables had been placed in a circle to allow for dancing afterward.

Right after dessert, Pam and her father, Bill, had the first dance. Joe and his mother joined in a couple of minutes later. Then the band's singer opened up the dance floor and got the party started!

Two hours before the reception ended, Joe and Pam cut the first pieces of cake and shared them. The cake was then passed on trays to the guest tables alongside other fun sweets for guests that wanted a sugar boost after dancing for a while. Pam threw her bouquet, and one of the bridesmaids caught it. Joe did the garter toss, and his first cousin, Tom, caught it.

Lots of bitesize snacks were placed on the buffet at this point to refuel guests; Dora and Joan brought them out. Joe and Pam were ready to leave, and the guests started lining up about ten minutes before they left getting ready to throw rice at the bride and groom and wish them the happiest lives together. Joe and Pam ran to the carriage with rice all over them. The carriage was decorated with flowers and more. Joe was so glad to have Pam to himself.

Joe had an all-inclusive honeymoon planned. It was romantic and stress-free. He wanted the honeymoon to be a surprise, so he asked Pam's mom to pack her luggage. He wouldn't tell her where they were going until they were on the train.

It was very cool to have the element of surprise. He planted false hints all over the place for her. It was kind of fun. They just wanted to enjoy being married.

Joe had taken Pam on the Princess Streamline boat. It was a journey that they would remember for the rest of their lives. It was a couple's paradise. They lay in each other's arms enjoying the sights of the water before they headed to their room where they enjoyed each other. They had one of the great Princess suites with a large bed and a private furnished balcony. The room was close to the restaurants with breathtaking views of the Mississippi. The romantic ambiance was off the charts. Every night they sat on the patio drinking wine and listening to the water as Joe held Pam in his arms.

"Let's go shopping for swimsuits," Joe said to Pam.

The boat had a gift shop, and they both went back to their room and changed into their suits. Joe and Pam were crazy about the water and loved to swim. Joe grabbed two towels, took Pam's hand, and walked out to a lounge chair for two. As Pam settled herself in Joe's arms Joe kissed her on the lips before telling her how happy he was to have her as his wife.

They loved the Princess; even though there were scattered thunderstorms throughout the week it was as close to a perfect honeymoon as they could get. They were so busy loving each other that they barely noticed the storms. Often, they would grab a drink and hang out on their private balcony and watch the water, land, and birds go by. The Princess was beautiful, and the room was lovely.

Pam and Joe went to one of the several nice restaurants and ordered steak and shrimp with white wine. The moment they arrived the waiter greeted them with a smile. They ordered and it wasn't long before the waiter returned with wonderful-looking food for them to enjoy. The food was delicious, and the waiter was there for them every few minutes.

"We had a great time, and the food was extra delicious," Joe told the waiter as he left a tip on the table. He took Pam's hand and walked out with his arm around her waist.

On the last night of their honeymoon on the Princess, the staff went above and beyond to make their dining experience special. Chef Jenny prepared an exquisite meal, and Alejandro, the waiter, was great. Joe and Pam loved the way the boat looked. The lodge was very well-kept, and housekeeping did a great job of keeping the rooms clean. Before leaving they told them they would be back next year.

Joe told them, "Thank you all from the bottom of our hearts. Our trip was more than we could have ever imagined."

Joe and Pam got on the train at the dock, and all the way home talked about what a great honeymoon they had.

Jim met them at the station, and as they rode home in the carriage, they pulled the shades down for a romantic night. Jim pulled up in front of the plantation but didn't get down until Joe opened the carriage door. Joe and Pam were having a last-minute honeymoon moment in the carriage.

Joe helped Pam down from the carriage and told Jim to bring in their luggage. Joe took Pam's arm and slowly walked her up the steps. When they reached the staircase, he carried Pam up the stairs, over the threshold, and into their bedroom where he closed the door with his foot.

CHAPTER SIXTEEN

THANK YOU NOTES

The next morning Pam was lying in Joe's arms not wanting to get up. Joe had brought her coffee and kissed her, "morning" as he got back in bed. As Joe kissed Pam, her hair fell over his chest. It was an hour before they finally pulled away from each other and got out of bed and went to have a shower.

When Joe was downstairs, he told Jane not to cook breakfast for them. He returned upstairs and no one saw them until dinner time. Jane had just finished preparing dinner for them and had brought the food to the table with hot coffee. They were both starved as they hadn't eaten since dinner yesterday, and everything looked great.

As they finished, Joe told Pam he was going to his office to write a thank you note to the resort. He leaned over and passionately kissed her before leaving.

Joe sat down at his desk and pulled out a piece of paper and a pen from his drawer.

Dear friends.

We just want to let you know how much Pam and I appreciated all you did for us on our honeymoon. You truly went above and beyond for us when we needed you. Our honeymoon was unbelievably perfect and magical. We would love to be able to go back again and again! We ate so much, and it was delicious!!! A smaller, more intimate honeymoon is exactly what we wanted after the wedding week. We spent every day enjoying the boat and water! We would recommend the Princess to anyone who's looking to plan a destination wedding and honeymoon. Thank you for being wonderful!

Sincerely, Joe and Pam Jenkins."

Joe went and told Pam, "Let's take a ride down by the river."

Pam and Joe walked out of the front, mounted their horses, and rode down the path in the back. They briefly stopped by the fence to allow the horses to graze. Joe reached down and picked a flower for Pam's hair and placed it behind her ear as he kissed her very loveably on her lips. They got off the horses and walked down to the river to sit on a log. He put his hand inside her dress and caressed her breast; he became extremely hot and slowly took Pam's hand and walked toward the woods. As they came upon a clean place, Joe pulled Pam down, smiling, and removed her dress. Pam was so beautiful, and Joe couldn't keep his hands off her.

Joe made mad love to her and told her he would love her for the rest of his life. Joe helped her put her dress back on and slowly walked to the horses, he placed a kiss on Pam's neck as they walked.

As they rode back to the house in silence it started to snow. Pam stared at the moon and the stars and the thousands of vivid reflections they created on the snow. Joe stared at her, looking at the way the moonlight lit her hair and softened her face. It was as if she had been created by magical fairies, so unearthly and glowing did she appear. It warmed Joe's heart to know she was his wife. It thrilled his soul to have a sudden feeling of excitement and pleasure to see her laugh and play tonight, with it snowing all around them. Joe noticed it produced a dazzling change in her and showed how she felt about him. It made his heart yearn for things he had never felt before with her. Only this woman, his wife, was the only one whose poise, grace, and charm could cause his heart to race. A thousand thoughts rushed through Joe's head as he rode silently beside her. Thoughts, feelings, and emotions surged through him in such a way that it almost made him shudder as he took her hand and rode toward home. He had given himself to many women, but he had never surrendered his heart to one woman as he had to Pam. Joe remained silent his heart beating so tumultuously that he felt it in his throat. Surely, she could hear his heart with her hand on his shoulder. Pam leaned over from her horse and began to brush the snow from his back and shoulder, and it nearly unseated him. He couldn't wait to get Pam home and in their bed.

As they rode, Pam asked him," What shall Jane think of us with snow all over us coming into the house?" Her voice was light and full of laughter as she swept away the traces of white from Joe's coat.

"Not her mind," he told her hastily as he pulled his horse to a stop, "that we are crazy and in love."

Pam's fingers were still upon his shoulder, and she looked up at him, laughing, and told him, "Let's go inside."

He brought his hand up and touched her cheek softly as if he was touching a rare treasure, he had long admired from afar. There was no perhaps about it, just wild, passion as he looked into her eyes and told her, "I will race you upstairs." They went inside and ran up the stairs hand in hand.

As Joe and Pam lay in their bed, it seemed like the night closed in around them, shutting out the whole world. Joe bent over her and briefly pressed his lips upon hers as he took her in his arms and held her tight.

The next morning Pam didn't want to get out of bed as she looked up at Joe with clear, green eyes and told him she must send out thank you cards.

Joe kissed her and told her, "Go ahead. I have a meeting to go to," as he climbed out of bed.

One of her bridesmaids had taken a photo of each gift after opening it to make it easier to reference the gift with the person giving it to them. It took Pam two days to write all of them. She placed them on the table downstairs reminding herself to tell Jim to take the cards to town to mail for her.

Pam's friend came by and wanted to know all about the honeymoon.

"Our honeymoon was fun and relaxing, after months of stress and planning a huge wedding, we laid on the deck, drank, ate a lot, and ... well, you know, we 'honeymooned," Pam said. "Just waking up together made my honeymoon special. We like food, and one particular night after coming back from one of the restaurants, a stranger giggled at us and said, "Honeymooners? We say," Yes, how can you tell?" He told us that they saw them in the restaurant, and he had never seen anyone look so much in love. It was small and maybe meaningless to anyone else, but it's something I will never forget. That makes it special."

"Having my husband to myself and no other distractions was pretty special. The couple's massages were amazing. We were in the same beautifully appointed room for our massage. We understand this can be strange for some, especially if this is your first time receiving dual treatment. It was a blissful, relaxing time for both of us. The room was almost twice the size of the other treatment rooms we have been to. It felt like we were in heaven. We enjoyed this crazy great treat."

"The people that ran the massage business told us not to have anything heavy to eat before our treatment. They said it would be best to have a light, healthy meal like a salad with a little protein a couple of hours beforehand. The lighter meal was supposed to give our food time to digest before the full-body massage."

"I felt shy when they first told me I would be in my birthday suit under the big spa blanket. My massage person told me not to worry. She told me that I would be always draped discreetly. Joe and I were so relaxed afterward we wanted to go again. The excursion we chose was swimming with just the two of us."

Pam became excited as she told May about swimming with the fish. She said it was an intimate, romantic, and life-changing experience that both of them could share. Just the two of them swimming and playing with fish in the warm waters! She explained that they were allowed to swim for a full hour in the water while the boat was stopped.

"Just the very idea of waking up whenever the mood strikes, lounging around with coffee (and sneaking in kisses because, you know, you're married, who cares?), and flat-out relaxing for two weeks for our honeymoon was heaven to us. "

"We were sitting on the dock during a Mississippi sunset. A perfect way to end our honeymoon trip. There was peaceful water behind us, warm temperatures, and other alluring details. But the one thing that may have impressed us the most is the mesmerizing sunset. The vibrant mix of yellows, reds, and oranges, sinking into the Mississippi, is unlike anything we have ever witnessed. May, the unique feature of this sunset from this spot is that it has an orange hue. The combination of the hues and the depth of the sunset was amazing. The evening in Jackson was peaceful, stimulating, and romantic all at the same time. We were on the Southeast side of the city and had the best view. "

"After months and months of wedding planning and meticulously checking boxes, and working towards one major culmination moment, it's over, in one blindingly beautiful whirl of love, emotion, and floral arrangements, the big day has come and gone. We recite our vows, party the night away with loved ones, and melt away the stress of it all on our honeymoon."

A few days later, while Pam was getting dressed, she wondered to herself, how do you come down from all of that and continue back into normal life, as a newlywed no less, and someone living with you? Pam knew some things were bound to surprise her. Just like the up and down emotions she felt in the days and weeks leading up to her wedding day, she was experiencing a wide range of emotions during her first week of marriage. Her emotions were ranging from excitement to anticipation to trepidation and even a sense of anti-climax. Pam loved Joe, but she didn't want sex all day long; she wasn't used to this. What is perhaps even more interesting was the fact that Joe didn't share the same emotion. She knew sexual access was likely to be a big deal right after the wedding.

Pam talked to May about it one morning after breakfast, and May told her, 'The bliss of the wedding is gone. No matter how long you've been together. It seems that having that piece of paper comes loaded with expectations. And you may find Joe doesn't meet with each one."

It had only been a couple of weeks and Joe was already busy working all the time. Pam had been the center of attention for so now she felt it was time to unpack her bags and return to the humdrum of everyday life many months, and with a mountain of things to crank out, to boot.

May told her, "Starting after you get married, your marriage grows into deeper, stronger, and steadier feelings for each other. By tuning out the world and focusing so intensely on each other, you're getting to know yourselves in your new roles as married partners. So, enjoy this sweet time of cocooning, just the two of you, and remember that it's vital to building a strong foundation for your family to come."

"You will have a really big fight," May said. "Whether it erupts while you're still on your honeymoon or as you unpack into your new shared home, The first big fight can be very frightening for you and Joe. After all, you may think, isn't this supposed to be the happiest time of our life? But bickering for the first time since you tied the knot is all but inevitable. You are two separate people, and you can now begin to work with those differences toward a common goal."

As Pam was coming down the stairs, she was thinking about all May had told her. She learned a lot from May.

CHAPTER SEVENTEEN

JANE'S FAMILY ROOTS

Jane had been working in Master Jenkins' home for over twelve years in the kitchen. One morning after breakfast she had a few minutes to spare and sat down and had a talk with Dora.

"In all reality, slavery is the source of a rich man's life. Master Jenkins and Miss Pam own over one thousand acres, a self-sustaining plantation that relies completely upon the labor of enslaved African American men, women, and children. The slaves perform the hard labor that produces Jenkins's cash crop, cotton. The more land Joe Jenkin accrues, the more slaves he procures to work it"

.

"Thus, the Jenkins family's survival is possible by the profit garnered from the crops that they enslave people to work daily on. When Joe bought Jenkins Plantation in 1842, he owned a hundred enslaved men, women, and children. Twenty years later, through both purchase and reproduction, that number has doubled." Jane told Dora, "He and Miss Pam own two hundred and seventy-five slaves who live and work on this property."

"When we came to Jenkins's plantation, it was encouraged for slaves to form family units. This was common with most slave owners. No slave can legally marry, but the creation of enslaved coupling like horses of African American men and women in plantation "marriages" allowed for the creation of enslaved families. No slave can vote, talk back to the white people, go to the front door, or live in the big house unless told to. These rules or laws were made to discourage slaves from attempting escape, as it would be much more difficult for an entire family to flee from captivity safely. Runaways are whipped in front of all their family if caught."

"Since many slaves are sold from their family; there is very little known about many of their family trees."

Dora was only three years old and was the youngest child on the plantation when Joe Jenkins purchased her family in 1853. Jim and Jane were given names by their original owner and did not have surnames. They called themselves "Shell" for their last name. Jane became head of the "house servants."

Jim was a trained blacksmith and carpenter, which was an important position on the plantation. The two jumped over the broom and married around 1849 and one year later Dora Ann Shell, their only child, was born.

Jane told Dora and Joan, "In some ways enslaved African American families very much resemble other families who live in other times, places, and under vastly different circumstances. Some slave husbands and wives love each other; some do not get along. Children sometimes abide by their parents' rules; other times, they follow their minds and get in trouble with their masters. In some critical ways, though, slavery marks everything about their lives making these families very different. Belonging to another human being brings disruptions, frustrations, and pain."

Jane said, "I have never known a whole family to live together, till all grown up, in my lifetime. Every family is separated due to sale, escape, and early death from poor health, suicide, and murder by a slaveholder, overseer, slave stroller, or another dominant person. There is also separation within the plantation itself by segregating "field slaves" from "house servants," removing children from their parents to live together with a slave caretaker, or bringing children fathered by the slaveholder to live in the "big house."

"How, then, does the slave family provide solace and identity?" asked Dora.

"What the family has done is created a world outside of the world of work. It allows a male slave to be more than just a brute beast. It allows him to be a father, to be a son. It allows women to be mothers and to take on roles that are outside of that of a slave, of a servant."

Dora asked Jane, "At what age did I realize how I live differently from the slaveholder?"

"You were about four when we were bought, it was then that you knew."

"Slaves are not to be happy. The family must stand on the auction block and be sold and separated from their children or each other. Slaves must stand on the auction block and hear the auctioneer's voice selling them away from the folks they love. Slave families represent a wide range of experiences: family separation and reunion, voluntary and forced marriages, the slave who knows all or none of their close kin, a mother who abandons her infant, and a voluntary father re-enslaved. To be with his son."

"Now we need to get up and clean the dining room of dishes," Jane told Dora.

While they were back in the kitchen and cleaning dishes, Jane talked to Dora about her Uncle Joe leaving them a mansion. and how Master Joe agreed to sign their freedom papers at the lawyer's office and let Joan go with them.

Dora stopped and looked at her mother, her mouth wide open. She couldn't believe it, all her fifteen years, she had been a slave, not free. Dora couldn't decide which one she was more excited about - the home or being free.

Jane told her, "I couldn't believe it either until I walked into our home."

Jane went out to the backyard to talk to Sue and Sally to tell them her great news. Sally and Sue were just coming up the hill from working in the cotton field when they saw Jane running down the hill waving her hands in the air with a big smile on her face. They didn't know what in the world Jane was so excited about, but she was smiling.

"Lord help me, my family is going to get our freedom, it is a beautiful day, and that is not all! Come sit down with me and let me tell you, hurry, I am just about to burst with excitement, and I got to tell someone."

Sally and Sue hurried over to the old chairs by the washroom and sat down.

Sally told Jane, "Tell us, girl."

Jane began by telling them how the lawyer knocked on the back door and how her uncle had left her a mansion on a hill. She told them it was down by the river and had a huge pond in the back. She explained that she and Jim had traveled to the lawyer's office before he took them to show them their new home.

"Mr. Wells wrote Master Joe a letter for our freedom. And best of all, ladies, we will be free after all these years; can you believe it? God has had a hand in this; I know it. I have been praying for this all my life, and now I can't believe it."

Sally and Sue hugged her and wished her happiness.

Jane told them, "One more thing, Master Joe is going to let Joan go with us."

Jane had to cook lunch for Master Jenkins and Mistress Pam. She told her friends, bye, and walked back into the house and to the kitchen. As she pulled out pans, she wondered to herself, how it would feel to shed the status of "slave" and become free. Many secure their freedom through escape, self-purchase, or being freed by the slaveholder. Now an uncle she had never met gave her and her family his home, and now they would have their freedom. She was thankful to God that after Master Joe signed the papers, her family would be free.

She couldn't believe she would get to walk down the street like a white woman with everyone telling her "hello" as she shopped. Master Joe had been good to them, but Jane had worked for white people that beat her and whipped her for no reason at all. She never wanted Dora to go through that.

Mr. Wells came by Jenkins Plantation and knocked on the back door again. Jane answered the door and invited him in.

"Mr. Wells, would you like to sit down and have a cup of coffee?"

After Mr. Wells and Jane sat down at the table, Mr. Wells smiled at her and pulled out papers Master Joe has signed for her family's freedom, but not Joan's.

"Joan will be able to go with you but doesn't get her freedom papers," he explained.

Jane was excited for her family but not so for Joan. She was going to have to tell Joan when she came into the kitchen for her lunch.

Mr. Wells told her, "In two weeks, the home will be yours; you and your family will be free to move in."

Joan came into the kitchen just as Mr. Wells was riding off.

Jane told her to sit down. "I have some good news and some bad news. You will be moving in with us in two weeks, but you do not get your freedom papers."

Joan was sad about not getting her freedom papers. She started crying and hitting the table with her fist "I can't believe it," she said. "I have been with Master Jenkins for six years and work hard at everything he asks. This is not fair; I am going to sue him." Joan has heard a lot about "the rights of man."

Joan wrote a letter to Mr. Wells to tell him that she wanted to sue Master Joe for her freedom.

Mr. Wells wrote back and asked her, "What has put such an extraordinary idea into your head?" Being satisfied by her reply, the lawyer agreed to represent her.

Mr. Wells knew the case was a reminder that slavery existed even in the cradle of abolitionism; it was a testament to the hopes inspired by revolutionary rhetoric. Joan was determined to be free. Mr. Wells had been a lawyer for ten years and knew it wouldn't be an easy case.

Mr. Wells wrote Joan a letter saying he wanted her to come to his office in Vicksburg, Mississippi, with Jim and Jane on Tuesday so he could talk to her.

Joan had heard that The First Article of the Declaration of Rights on the new constitution stated that "all men are born free and equal, and have certain natural, essential, and inalienable rights." She was told, "that the sentiments expressed by the Sheffield Declaration and the Declaration of Independence are now the law of the state and county in which she lived and worked."

Joan told Mr. Wells, "I am a dramatic woman, and I have a right to be free." She told him that she had decided that the time had come to put these high-sounding words to the test.

Mr. Wells wrote Master Jenkins a letter telling him, Joan had filed to sue him for her freedom. When Jim brought the mail from town and handed it to Master Joe in his office Joe saw the envelope with the lawyer's name on it and figured it had something to do with Jane and Jim's case. He was surprised when he read the first line of the letter stating that Joan was suing him for her freedom.

Joe found Pam in the knitting room and sat down with her to talk. Joe purchased Joan when she was eleven, six years ago, and was happy with her work. He didn't want to lose her as a house hand and give her freedom.

Pam put her hand on his arm and asked him, "Would you like to be a slave?"

Joe just looked at her and told her, "No. No."

The next morning Joe wrote to Mr. Wells and told him that he would give Joan her freedom to work for Jim and Jane Shell for two hundred dollars. After sending the letter he called Jim and Jane into his office and told them if they paid him the two hundred dollars, he would sign the papers for Joan's freedom. The couple agreed to the terms and sat down and wrote a letter to Mr. Wells explaining their plans for Joan.

Mr. Wells wrote to Joe and asked him to come to the meeting on Tuesday so that he could sign the papers.

Tuesday morning, Jim brought the carriage around to the front steps for Joe and Pam. Joan and Jane followed in a wagon behind. They wanted to do some shopping after their appointment with the lawyer.

Everyone pulled up to the lawyer's office, and Jim and Joe helped the ladies down. Mr. Wells opened his door as Joe stepped down from the carriage; he invited everyone in.

"Get coffee for everyone," Mr. Wells told his secretary as he led them to his office. He told everyone to have a seat before he walked around the desk and sat in his chair.

As he picked up the papers in front of him, he looked at Joan and told her, "Free black people still face danger. Many appear in court to ask for a Certificate of Freedom. This paper is what I am giving you today, Joan, signed by Joe Jenkins for your freedom. Jim and Jane are putting up the two hundred dollars for me to hold for two weeks when you move in with them. When you are eighteen, you are to be paid a salary and give them back half of the money each month until the two hundred dollars is paid back to them, and then you will be free to go where you want. We are all hoping you will stay working for Jim and Jane for a long time. As you know, they are good people and will always be fair to you."

"Freedom papers and certificates for freedom are documents declaring the free status of blacks. These papers are important because "free people of color" live with the constant fear of being kidnapped and sold into slavery as you know. Freedom papers prove the free status of a person and serve as a legal affidavit. Put these in a safe place, Joan. If for some reason you lose them, let me know."

"Filing with the deeds office protects African Americans from the loss, theft, or destruction of original documents, as in all-too-frequent situations where slave catchers confiscate or destroy freedom papers to force free men and women into the lives of bondage."

Mr. Wells handed the papers around for everyone to sign and stood up and thanked them all for coming in.

"I just didn't want to lose you, but Jim and Jane are great people. Be sure and come see Pam and me soon," Joe told Joan.

Joan was excited she was going to be free for the rest of her life. She had never known freedom before, and she didn't know how to feel.

Pam and Joe walked out and shook Mr. Well's hand and told him to come to their next dinner.

Jim was taking Joe and Pam home in the carriage. Jane and Joan had their freedom papers on top of their dress safe in case they needed them. They walked down the sidewalk looking at dressings in the window.

"I am going to make myself a freedom dress just like that one in the window when I get home," Joan told Jane.

Jane laughed at her and told her, "Make me one too, in a different color."

They both walked into a fabric store to buy fabric and thread for the dresses. When the owner saw them, he didn't smile but told the ladies that he would wait on them in the back.

"I will get my papers out here and show you the freedom papers I have just gotten," Joan said.

The owner walked over and looked at the papers and then looked at the two women. After confirming the papers were real he told the lady working in the store to hurry up and cut the fabric so the two women would leave.

When Joan and Jane got back out on the sidewalk, they laughed about what an idiot the man was. They returned home to Jenkins Plantation.

Joan went to her shack and started cutting out a beautiful everyday dress. It was going to be red with little white flowers and butterflies. Joan worked late into the night and had it done in time to wear the next day. She got up at five in the morning and tried it on. It was perfect. She put her hair on her head and slipped on her shoes before going down to show Jane. Jane was in the kitchen cooking by the stove when Joan came in.

"Well, look at you, how beautiful you look this morning," Jane said "I want mine just like it by tomorrow morning."

Joan and Jane had become particularly good friends and would do anything for each other. Jane was so glad Joan had her freedom papers and would be moving in with her and her family next week.

"Let's bake a cake and celebrate our freedom," Jane told Joan.

They hugged each other before Joan put on her apron and started making a cake.

CHAPTER EIGHTEEN

LOOKING AT THEIR NEW HOME

Jim, Jane, and Dora were excited. Mr. Wells handed them the papers for Jane's uncle's estate, and now they owned a thirty- two thousand square foot home. It was a long way from their one-room shacks. Jane sat in her Master Jenkins' kitchen and read the words written on the pages three times. She still couldn't believe it. The mansion was three stories and had a large round room at the top to look out over their ninety acres as far as they could see.

Jim went out and pulled the wagon to the front and helped Jane, Dora, and Joan step up into the wagon. The mansion was fifteen miles from where they lived now and would take a while to get there. Jane had a picnic basket and water to take and eat by the lake. She handed it to Jim to put in the back of the wagon for a picnic on the way. It was a beautiful day, and the sun was bright. Jane had her umbrella up over her head, so the sun wouldn't blind her.

Jim knew of a lake by the road, and when they came upon it, Jim pulled over and helped everyone down. Jane looked over toward the lake. They had never been allowed to picnic. Jane wanted to cry. It was like going to "heaven." They were free! Jane felt funny about it, but she laid the tablecloth on the ground and pulled the basket out of the wagon. Everyone enjoyed fried chicken, potato salad, and pie.

"I am going to lay down for a nap," Jim told her. But the girls couldn't wait to see their new home. They still had five miles to go, and they couldn't wait. They pulled him up from the ground wanting to go. He laughed at them and stood up and everyone got back in the wagon. They were on their way.

Jim rode up to the forest of trees and turned down a road to the right. As they came down the drive, Dora saw the house. Dora was so excited she couldn't wait and jumped off the back of the wagon, running toward the house to the large front porch. It was big enough to dance on, and she did just so. She was like a little kid laughing and turning around and dancing.

Jim pulled up to the front door in the wagon and helped Jane down. Joan jumped off and went to the porch where Dora was, and they hugged each other. They couldn't believe their eyes at how big the house was, and the yard was huge. Jane walked up to the porch. Everywhere she looked in the house were column posts and a fence along the front and sides.

Jane was so excited she told them, "Let's go inside."

They had never been allowed to enter the house through the front door but this was their home and they couldn't wait. Jim took Jane's arm as they walked through the double doors. To the right was a large living room with a fireplace, and all the rooms were furnished. Jim and Jane were glad about this; they didn't have to buy furniture.

Dora and Joan were just amazed as they walked around the large living room. They had never in their lives lived in a huge home. Past the large living room was the dining room right off the kitchen. A large, beautiful table was in the center with twelve lovely chairs. Jane was afraid to touch anything; it was like a dream. As she walked over to the china cabinet, she saw beautiful china inside, all just alike. A large buffet was across the room with a large mirror on top. Jane opened the drawers of the buffet, and tablecloths, silverware, and more were all laid in order. Everything was all set up for them to move in. There were hardwood floors throughout the home.

Jane looked at Dora and Joan and told them, "Both of you have your work cut out for you cleaning every day. "

Dora and Joan looked at Jane and told her, "We will love it. It is all ours!" They ran over to Jane and grabbed her hands. "Let's look around."

Jim walked over to one of the many fireplaces and told Jane, "I guess I will be cutting a lot of firewood." He laughed as he took Jane in his arms.

Dora pointed toward the top of the ceiling. It was round with windows everywhere and a walkway with rails all the way around.

"I will race you to the top," Dora told Joan and they ran up the eighteen stairs. As the girls were upstairs going from room to room picking out their bedrooms Jim and Jane walked upstairs checking out the second and third floors. In addition to luxurious bedrooms, there were areas where guests once played parlor games and took afternoon tea by the windows overlooking the ninety acres.

The fourth floor featured maids' bedrooms and the observatory with spectacular views from the front of the house.

Mr. Wells had told them, "Downstairs, the domestic servants keep the entire house running smoothly with the help of a state-of-the-art domestic nerve center complex with the main kitchen, two specialty kitchens, a large laundry complex, refrigeration systems, and pantries."

Jane couldn't believe the kitchen as she walked through; it was the most beautiful kitchen she had ever seen. There were two kitchens. The large kitchen had a beautiful table and a cutting table in the middle with a huge stove, marble floor, sink with running water, and water heater, so she didn't have to go out in the cold to pump water; large refrigeration full of food and pantries all over with enough food for an army.

Jane's uncle wanted his mountain home to provide family and friends with recreational pleasures and an indoor bathroom with running water. Jane went into the master bathroom and sat down in the tub. She wanted to sit there for the rest of her life.

"It is big enough for three people," she told Jim.

Jim laughed at her and helped her out, telling her, "We have a lot more to see."

They went outside and walked onto the library terrace and gazed below into the gardens with beautiful roses of all colors. Jane told Jim," Oh, Jim, just look at all the beautiful roses. I just love roses."

As they looked out the back, they could see rare Franklinian and Persian ironwood trees growing side by side with mountain laurel, rhododendron, native azaleas, and white pine. It was all theirs. Jim looked over to the left and showed Jane a four-acre garden. It featured twenty-five thousand tulips each spring, summer annuals in warmer months, and chrysanthemums in the autumn, as well as an All-American Rose Garden. Jane couldn't wait to walk through the flower garden and run down the hill to smell some of them. She had tears in her eyes as Jim came up behind her and took her in his arms. As she looked up at him, he was crying too.

"We are going to have to hire men and women to help us with this big place; we can't do it all by ourselves. I know your uncle has people working for him. We will have to get a list of names from Mr. Wells," Jim said to Jane.

Jim went to find the girls. "We have to go back and get in the wagon as it is getting late."

"What a dream come true," Jane said.

The next morning Jane and the girls started packing and throwing away things they didn't want to move with them. Jane went through Jim's clothes and sewed any holes he had in them; then, she looked at her clothes. She didn't have but two dresses plus the one Joan was making her; but now, with the money her uncle had left her, she could buy some fabric and have Joan make her and Dora a couple more.

Joan worked until midnight on Jane's dress and had it done. She couldn't wait to bring it into the kitchen the next morning to give it to Jane. It was just like hers but green. Joan started up the steps and called out Jane's name. Jane was at the sink washing pots and pans from breakfast. When Jane turned around, Joan had the dress up in front of her chest, smiling at Jane. Jane ran over and took the dress from her.

She was so excited. "Thank you," she told Joan and ran downstairs to try it on. Jane was laughing all the way down the steps. She ran into her room, pulled off her old torn-up house dress, and slowly put the lovely green dress on, smoothing out any wrinkles. She walked over to the broken mirror and looked at herself. She turned around, looking at the back, she didn't know how a queen felt, but she was just that proud of the dress.

Jane walked back up the steps and hugged Joan's neck. Jane said, "This is the prettiest thing I have ever owned," with tears in her eyes. "I better go and take this beautiful dress off. I don't want to get flour all over it. I can wear it the day I move and to church."

At this time Jane and the girls were still working for Master Joe. Jane said, "We better get to cooking dinner." Jane was making buttermilk fried chicken with honey butter biscuits along with cooked carrots and homemade white gravy.

"Peel the carrots," she told Dora. Jane went to the fridge and pulled out the buttermilk, hot pepper sauce, four pounds of frying chicken, all-purpose flour, salt, dried thyme leaves, freshly ground black pepper, nutmeg, and oil for frying, about three cups. After she had it all on the cutting table, she checked everything off.

Jane told Joan to go ahead and roll out the batter to make the biscuits. While Joan was making the biscuit batter and rolling it out, Jane started the buttermilk fried chicken. Jane pulled out a large bowl after washing the chicken off. She measured one cup of buttermilk, half a teaspoon of hot pepper sauce, one cup of all-purpose flour, one teaspoon of salt, one teaspoon of dried thyme leaves, half a teaspoon of freshly ground black pepper, one-eight teaspoons of nutmeg. She had three cups of oil for frying and heating on the stove. She mixed all the ingredients in the bowl, cut the chicken up, dusted the chicken in the bowl, and laid the chicken in the hot grease one piece at a time. She reserved three tablespoons of the flour mixture for the gravy and set it to the side to make after the chicken was almost done.

Joan had the biscuits in the pan and put them in the oven. Dora had the carrots on low on the back burner to cook. Jane told Dora and Joan, "I will watch the food while you two set the dining room table for two. Be sure and put a nice clean tablecloth on the table this time," she said as she looked at the girls. Jane had found a small spot on the last one they put on. Jane looked up at them and told them, "Don't forget fresh flowers for the table."

The chicken came out looking great to Jane. She poured the gravy into a gravy bowl and told Dora to put it on the table with the chicken. Jane took the biscuits out of the oven and poured the carrots into a bowl and gave them to Joan to carry out to the table. Joan had picked some black eye peas for Jane that morning out of the garden, poured them into a bowl, and carried them to the table. Jane went into the dining room right before Joe walked in with Pam on his arm. Jane looked around to make sure the girls did a great job this time.

As Joe walked in, he told Pam, "Something smells good, and I can't wait to eat. Jane always cooks the best food." Jane heard him from the kitchen, and a smile came to her face. She would miss cooking for him, but she was excited to be having her own home soon.

Joe talked to Pam, "We need someone to run the house and replace Jane, Jim, and Dora." He handed Pam a piece of paper with his ad in the newspaper – Wanted! Strong woman for cooking in the kitchen, able to bake, wash, milk, and feed calves; and run a house." Joe told her, "We also need two more girls to work in the house and fields." His second ad said, "Wanted. Two strong, steady girls who can cook, clean, and work in the fields for room and board."

Joe was always working in the office running his plantation or in town talking to businessmen. He needed Pam's help in running the home. Pam was familiar with running a plantation home as she helped her mother run their home before marrying Joe. She enjoyed riding horses, gardening, sewing, playing the spinet, and dancing.

At the age of seventeen, Pam started dating Joe Jenkins, and they were married by the time she was eighteen. Pam knew what to do and took over the Jenkins plantation running the house, while her husband managed the estate, encompassing over one thousand acres. Joe adored Pam, she was smart, pretty, and young, and he pampered her with the finest clothes and gifts he imported from Paris.

Pam's early education proved quite helpful in the plantation operation, and she consulted with her husband and lawyers when she felt it was necessary. It took a lot of money to run a plantation; Joe and Pam's home had turrets, a ballroom, a maze in the garden, five bedrooms, and fields for cotton. Pam had to make sure the kitchen was run right, the garden was kept nice, the house was clean, and food was on the table for them and the slaves in the big house. There were thirty-two one-room row houses for the slaves and their families.

Pam had to hire another man to replace Jim. Joe needed someone to work on the heating, keeping the roof in good repair, taking care of the animals, and mowing the lawns. She called Jim and Jane into her office, "Do either of you know of any good workers who can take your places?"

Jane told her, "Sue and Sally are very good at cooking and are great housekeepers."

Pam asked Jane, "Will you and the girls mind training them for a few days before you leave?"

Jane told her, "We will love to."

Pam called the ladies inside the office. Sue and Sally had never been inside the office before and didn't know what they had done. They walked down the hallway with edgy looks on their faces. Pam stepped out the door of the office and smiled at them. She told them, "Come on in and have a seat."

This was the first time anyone had asked them to have a seat in the big house. They looked first at Pam and then down at the chair before slowly sitting down.

Pam told them that she wanted them to work in the kitchen and clean the house. She explained that Jane recommended both of them for this work.

Sue and Sally looked at each other, momentarily stunned, then told Pam, "We will love to do this work."

Pam told them that they and their families would move to the big house to live downstairs in the kitchen quarters. They would have two rooms, each for their families to sleep in. They would eat their meal in the kitchen after Pam and Joe's meals. She asked them, "Will your husbands like to leave the fields working cotton and be our groundkeepers?"

Both Sally and Sue knew how hard their husbands worked and told Pam, "Yes, Ma'am." Sally and Sue couldn't wait for their husbands to come out of the field so they could tell them. Both men were excited and loved the change in jobs.

Pam knew, like her husband, that a wife had certain duties to safeguard the family. Most important of these, Pam knew that obeying her husband was a good deed. Her mother told her that one of the foremost commitments and chief duties toward her husband was to obey him in everything that is not unlawful. However, recently things had changed, and this was not necessarily the case. A husband was the head of the family and its guardian. He carried this responsibility because his physical makeup made him fit to carry the burdens of life and support his family. In the 1800s, it was obvious that obedience evinces a woman's capacity for good judgment and a realistic view of life. Every morning at breakfast, Joe and Pam discussed the plans for the day. Pam would have a list for Joe to look over, and she would carry out everything he told her to.

Pam kept the books on everything for Joe and brought the book with her at breakfast. Pam always tried to guard her honor as well as her husband's honor. Her mother told her she must never betray her husband nor forfeit his rights. She was entrusted to spend money on the house and herself wisely and manage her family's affairs in its best interest. Never spend her husband's money without his permission.

Joe reviewed Pam's list and told her, "Go ahead and let Jane train Sally and Sue. But they can't move in the quarters until Jim and Jane move out."

Pam instructed Jane to tell Sue and Sally to be in the kitchen ready to work at five. Jane enjoyed training the two ladies as they were very good cooks, and it didn't take long to prepare them for Master Joe and Miss Pam. Jane had Joan, and Dora train them on how to set the table and clean the house.

Pam had two more girls from the fields to wash, clean the house, and help in the kitchen when needed. Two slave girls, Cindy and Judy, were shown how to do the washing. Joan told them, "Make sure everything is clean before putting it back in the drawers at the big house." Dora showed them how to heat the water, put the clothes in the kettle, and stir them with the big stick.

CHAPTER NINETEEN

KITCHEN TRAINING

Jane sat up in bed; she reached over Jim to get her robe. It was five, and she was to train Sally and Sue today in the kitchen. She climbed over Jim and headed for the pitcher of water and poured some into her bowl to wash her face. Jane looked in the mirror one more time. She had been here for a long time, but soon she would be lying in her new bed in her new home. She was free, and it felt great.

Jane walked through the back door into the kitchen, stopped, and looked around. No one was there yet. She knew every inch of the room. Her fingerprints were on everything. She walked over and touched the stove she had been cooking on for years. She was a little sad that someone else was taking her place. Dora had been in this kitchen for twelve years. Where did the time go? She knew this would be the last day she would be cooking in this kitchen. Now she smiled as she got excited about moving to her nice home.

She heard a noise and turned around from the stove; Sally and Sue had just walked through the back door. Jane smiled at them, and the two ladies smiled back at her. They knew what Jane was thinking, and they walked over and hugged her. They told her, "We promise to take good care of your kitchen."

A tear fell slowly down Jane's cheek, and she hugged them back and told them, "You better!"

Jane started by showing them where the pots and pans were and told Sally to go to the pantry and get the flour out of the flour bin.

139

Sue was getting milk, eggs, and bacon from the fridge. Jane told them, "Pam and Joe are going horseback riding this morning and will be hungry when they come back."

Jane always cooked for Joe and Pam and all the slaves that worked for Joe. Sally and Sue both carried items to the table for the biscuits and started making the batter. As Sally worked on the dough, Sue started pinching off the dough and placed the pieces on the pans. Sue put the first three pans in the oven and then started preparing the next three.

Eggs were next. Jane told both ladies, "Grab the big skillet in the back of the cabinet. Get the lard and heat it for the eggs." Jane already had the bacon cooking and was putting more in two skillets.

Jane always made homemade jam. She asked them the two women, "Do either of you know how to make jam?"

Both ladies told her, "No."

"In July, I pick blackberries, and in April strawberries. These are only for Joe and Pam," Jane said. "Could you watch the food cooking while I go and show Sue how I set the table?" Jane asked Sally before the two women walked into the dining room.

Jane walked over to the buffet and opened the bottom drawer and removed two tablecloths. She told Sue that she always had an extra tablecloth for backup in case of spills. Jane handed Sue the tablecloth and told her to go ahead and place it on the table. Jane walked around to the other side to help her spread the tablecloth and smooth it with her hands. Next, they placed the second one on top of the first one and repeated the process.

Jane opened the top drawer and removed the silverware and napkins and showed Sue how to place the silverware on the table. Jane instructed Sue to open the china cabinet and bring the plates, butter dishes, and bowls. Next, Sue carefully removed the delicate, pretty cups from the china cabinet and placed them by the plates. Jane looked everything over and then grabbed a crystal vase.

"Every morning, there must be a vase with freshly cut flowers on the table. We need to go back to the kitchen and help Sally bring food to the table," Jane told Sue.

When Sue and Joan walked into the kitchen, Sally took the biscuits out of the oven and set the pans on top of the stove.

"We will take the food to the table when we hear Joe and Pam come in the front door. Now we have to go pick flowers." Jane secured the flower basket, and all of them walked out the back door to the side of the house. Jane stressed, "Never walk out the front door."

They picked a beautiful bouquet of pink, red, and yellow roses and brought them into the kitchen. Jane instructed them to place the roses on the cutting board, and she grabbed the crystal vase. Jane showed the ladies how low to cut the flowers before placing them in the vase. Jane told the ladies that the flowers had to be low enough so Joe and Pam could see over them. Jane handed Sue the vase with flowers and instructed her to place the vase in the middle of the table and make sure she didn't spill the water.

Pam and Joe arrived back from horseback riding and had just walked in the front door. Jane told the ladies, "That is our cue to take the food out to the table."

Sally picked up a plate of biscuits, and the gravy bowl while Sue brought the platter of eggs with bacon. Jane carried the coffee, sugar, and cream. After everything was on the table, Jane whispered to Sue to bring the jam to the table.

Joe and Pam were laughing on their way into the dining room. Joe pulled out Pam's chair and helped her be seated. Joe told the ladies, "Everything looks great. I am starved," as he handed Pam the bacon.

Joe and Pam finished their meal and went down to the barn as one of their mares was having her colt. Jim and one of the other slave men were helping the mare; she had a hard time but eventually gave birth to a black colt.

Pam and Joe returned to the house, and Joe had to go into town for a business meeting. Before, he left he reviewed Pam's list. She showed him that she spoke to Sally's husband John and Sue's husband Jerry about taking on the role of the groundskeeper. Cindy and Judy were two other girls to work in the fields and help clean the house and do the laundry. Joe looked over the list and told Pam, to go ahead and hire all of them.

Pam had a grocery list for food for the help and all the slaves' food. She told Joe, "It will cost you $24.00 per week to feed them."

Joe kissed her goodbye and walked out the front door to his horse that John brought around. He smiled to himself as he rode down the drive. He was a happy man.

Joe arrived in town, tied up Star, and walked over to the Pleasure Hotel for lunch and a business meeting. Walking into the hotel he informed the deskman of his arrival.

The deskman told him, "Yes, sir, Mr. Jenkins right this way. The other men are already ordering lunch."

In the mid-1850s, America was facing a political crisis. Joe was at the business meeting. Slavery was threatening to tear the nation apart, and what's worse, the Great Triumvirate - Senators Henry Clay, Daniel Webster, and John Calhoun, who had broken the peace and compromise for decades, were all gone. It was for a new generation of leaders. Joe and the men were at the meeting to discuss what could be done with these changes. America's people were thinking about accepting the idea of popular sovereignty; this meant new states would decide for themselves whether to accept or ban slavery. Joe and the men believed the whole process was wracked with fraud and violence. Abraham Lincoln, who was virtually an unknown Republican, was Douglas' opposition.

Joe and the other men supported Douglas. This year was an election year for the Illinois State House. Douglas wanted to enhance his chances of being chosen by campaigning for Democratic legislators.

"Douglas has a chance to win if his friends who run the railroad travel the States and give speeches," Joe told the men. "The only problem is that Lincoln will show up two days later and give voters reasons not to trust

Douglas. In other words, Lincoln will get the last word in and probably win."

"And who are we going to get to set up these meetings and check on Lincoln's schedule?" One man asked sarcastically.

Joe informed him that he had friends in Washington D.C. who would love to do the job.

True to his style, Lincoln religiously arrived two days after Douglas' meetings. Douglas agreed to finally meet Abraham Lincoln face to face in a series of debates in the remaining Congressional districts in the state. The businessmen made sure they were at the debates. There were seven Lincoln-Douglas debates, in which the two candidates for Senate squared off against each other, challenging each other's ideas about many topics but most importantly, slavery and its future in the United States. Even though these speeches were intended to help elect their respective parties' state legislators, they attracted tens of thousands of people.

"The audience turns the debates into a sporting event, shouting out questions, cheering, booing, and laughing at both men." Joe was standing in front of the men and was reading the front page of the Chicago newspaper. Joe read how the reporters in Chicago transcribed the speeches thanks to the telegraphs. The Lincoln-Douglas debates were reported by newspapers across the entire nation and followed closely by the American people. Joe told the men, "This is not good. I believe Lincoln can win."

Joe and the men were at one of the debates and heard Douglas tell Lincoln, "You, sir, are a radical abolitionist who wants to turn Illinois into a colony for free Blacks!"

Lincoln told him, "No, I'm not! You want to expand slavery across the entire nation!"

There were more people at the second debate. Lincoln spoke first, answering more direct questions that Douglas asked him at the previous debate. People from slave states showed up to cheer on Douglas and boo Lincoln.

'You say the country cannot exist half slave and half free?" Lincoln debated, "It seems that the Founding Fathers designed it that way and that the country has survived in this condition and has grown. Them's are fighting words when you say that we have to be all slaves or all free."

Joe sat and talked to the other men. He commented, "I am told that a Negro is not and never will be a citizen of the United States. This government is created on a white basis, by white men, for the benefit of white men and their posterity must forever be administered by white men and no others. This is what my father told me and what his father told him. Gentlemen, I am in favor of preserving this government as our fathers made it." Everyone in the meeting agreed with Joe, and they stand up and shook hands. As Joe rode Star to the front of his home, he thought " Was there going to be a war?"

CHAPTER TWENTY

GOOD TIMES ON THE OLD PLANTATION

Master Joe and Pam wanted to give Jim and his family a farewell get-together. Joe told Jim, "Tell the men and their families in the fields to come in at five from the fields. Pam and I want to give you and your family a going away party down by the river."

Sally, Sue, and Jane had been cooking food all day. The women in the row houses also brought their specialties. Mamas were scrubbing their children and putting them in their best clothes. The children were instructed not to get dirty or else … the children didn't understand why their mammas told them to keep clean and they got dirty anyway.

Black slaves living on a Southern plantation experienced oppression and dehumanization. Joe and Pam were good to their slaves. They never whipped them; instead, they would call them to the shed and talk to them. The slaves could maintain an essential spirit and a degree of contentment by creating different cultural forms. Master Joe only had only one slave run away in his twelve years as master.

Slaves' culture was reflected in their family life, socialization, religion, and recreational activities. They loved to sit around the fire at night and play an instrument, and dance. During those moments of unguarded merrymaking, the slave families often revealed their innermost selves and a great deal about the character of their being.

Sally, Jane, Joan, and Sue were in the kitchen cooking and wrapping up the food.

Sue asked the ladies, "Why don't we have a trade gathering? I will go and ask everyone to bring things they don't have any use for anymore and see if they want to put items on the trade table."

Jane commented that she had a couple of necklaces out of rocks she could add to the table.

Dora told them, "I can make two cakes and some cookies to trade."

Sue went door to door down the row of cabins and told everyone to spread the word.

The party for Jim and his family started at 5:00 in the evening, and everyone was attending. The men were retrieving the tables for the ladies' food. Jim and several of his friends found wood for the fire. Joe had hired a clown and singers to come to entertain at 6:00.

The ladies brought out the food and set everything on the tables. Someone had put lights in the trees. There were separate tables for all the trade items. Dora and Joan had never seen so many items to trade in their lives. Joan wasn't quite sure if the idea would take. They were both thrilled as they inspected many of the goods on the tables. Both of them knew that boys their age would be there and took extra care in making sure they looked their best in their new dresses.

As Dora and Joan were carrying food down to the river, a breeze blew the biting insects away. They were both excited to talk to boys. Joan didn't see any boys her age, but Dora told her, "It is early, and I know things will get better." Sure enough, both Dora and Joan had boys lined up, asking each of them to dance.

Several of the men had two pigs roastin' over the fire. Jim told his friend, "Master Joe wants to make sure we didn't run out of meat before the night was over."

Joan and Dora were behind the tables filling the children's plates first. The children were instructed to make a single line. Two little boys were pushing each other. Their daddy pulled their ears, straightening them up fast. Then the men were next in line. Everyone was having a great time eating and dancing. There was plenty of food for a second round. The ladies cooked more food to go with the pigs, frog legs, fresh fish, coon, ham, and turkey. Jim's nose was beginning to pick up different scents of food as he scanned the tables.

Everyone was sitting and enjoying talking to each other. A wagon came down the drive, a clown was waving, and two women were singing. The wagon stopped, and the clown jumped down and began dancing around the children and making balloons for each one of them. The children were laughing and dancing with them.

Three of the slave men pulled out their instruments and joined right in with the women singers. Men started standing up and taking their wives ' hands and leading them to the dance area. The step of every Negro dance that was ever known was called into requisition and admirably executed. The slaves danced the "double shuffle, and "the Virginly break-down," with ample applause and irresistible effect. Everyone on the sidelines was clapping and hollering for them. The women singers got everyone to sing, "Hoe Corn and Dig Potatoes." The slave ladies had hoes in their hands while they sang and danced.

Sally had homemade soap and candles to trade. It took a minute, but Sally began to see a long line forming by her table. It was madness! There was an outer ring of tables for hocking and trading goods. The inner circle was for talking and eating.

Some men started a wrestling competition, games of chance, board games, and dancing. Children ran past them, hollering wildly. Joe and Jim were standing, when John walked up to some men standing nearby and asked them if they knew where Jim was. Jim overheard the question, and yelled, "Hey, here I am," and waved at the men.

It was an interesting night. Some people were dancing, kids were playing kick-the-can, and everyone was looking over the trade items. The trade show was a great success with a rhyme and rhythm to the trading. Everyone needed items from kids' clothes to shoes for themselves. All of Dora's cakes and cookies were gone. A person trading her items might have thought that her things were worthless, but everything was going quickly.

Joan procured more fabric because she didn't have enough to make herself dresses. She traded a dress for more threads and needles. She stopped trading for a minute to walk over and ingest roasted pig, corn, and rice. A boy her age was standing in the line and asked if he could carry her plate for her. He told her about participating in games.

"Are you going to participate in the wrestling," she asked him.

"Wrestling looks like a dirty business. You can always tell which man has participated because he is covered in mud."

She laughed at him, and together they walked over to a log. As they walked, the boy told her, "My name is Jack," Jack asked her where she worked and if he could come to see her next week.

"You can come to see me, but I am moving soon." Joan then elaborated on her soon-to-be new home. Jack and Joan walked toward the river by the woods. Jack took her in his arms and softly kissed her goodnight.

Jack told her that he would help with the move as long as he had Master Joe's approval. He then walked her back to her booth.

One lady had a black wash kettle to trade. This wash kettle was made of hammered brass-trimmed with iron with a hand-forged iron bail. Another woman had knives her husband had made. Metal pocket knives had special importance for all men as they could use them to work with. Some of the knives could be worn in sheaths on the belt for immediate use. This lady also had knives for butchering and carving. The greatest utility of a knife is for skinning animals and cutting meat for their family's meals. Every knife warranted another item for trade.

Another lady had axes that she and her husband had made. All of their iron axes were available in different sizes and shapes. Her husband was a blacksmith. These axes were handy in cutting trees for firewood and cleaning paths and trails for hunting.

Some women made blankets out of everything from animal skins, and furs to scraps of clothes sewn together by hand. Some of the blankets were tanned and, in other cases, pelts were sewn together to serve as coats, with the fur worn on the inside.

At the end of the night, the ladies cleaned up all the remaining food, and the men put all the tables away and put out the fire. There were only a few items left on the trade tables. Everyone hugged Jim's family before retiring for the night.

As they lay in bed, Jim and Jane couldn't believe they were moving to their big house the next day. Everyone had been packing for two days. The wagon was loaded with all their belongings and ready to go.

By the time Jim, Jane, Dora, and Joan moved into the house in early 1861, Jim and Jane had been married sixteen years, Dora was fifteen, and Joan was seventeen. As Jim and Jane pulled up in front of their home, they never thought they would ever be free. Jim and Jane had never been homeowners. Jim was aware that he would have to hire a carpenter, cook, blacksmith, and possibly other skilled individuals to help run their plantation. Jim was aware that most slaves were common laborers.

At the earliest stage of plantation development, slaves, even common laborers, traditionally worked under the supervision of a foreman. Jim was going to need field hands to work the cotton fields and a foreman to delegate and supervise their work. He was also going to need field hands for the tobacco crops.

The home unit was comprised of the plantation mansion, outbuildings housing cooks and craftsmen, storage sheds, and a dock to receive supplies and ship off tobacco. Jim knew that he would need workers to work from sunrise to sunset with the planting, hoeing, harvesting, and preparing of the fields before and after these major events. He also knew that this hard routine work was unrelieved by many varieties. Jim required a foreman to have a watchful eye on an overseer. The overseer was the individual who sets the pace and reports unproductive workers to the foreman. There were still several slaves at the mansion, but many of them had left when Jane's uncle died.

Jim traveled to town and placed an ad in the newspaper outlining the labor he needed for the mansion. The next morning, after the paper came out, people arrived at the back of their estate to apply. Jim hired all thirteen slaves that showed up. He told Jane to show the cook where to put her belonging. Jim, in turn, showed all the men and their families where the row houses were.

Jim showed one man where the shed was for cutting wood and carpentry to fix the house. Jim hired Josh to cut lumber for Jim to sell. Josh had to work twelve hours a day, seven days a week; he got paid a dollar and a half a day. As a young man, Josh helped his father with farming chores and worked as a raftsman on the upstate waterways. Josh had lived closer to the land and understood the environment and lumber business better than Jim. Josh's knowledge was both intimate and precise on what to do. He knew how to use the forest environment for sustenance and sometimes as a tool for the logging business.

Josh came from Africa and was a part of the forest industry from the earliest colonial days. The sawmill Josh would work on was no more than a huge pit where one man stood at the top and another at the bottom as they sawed majestic logs into planks. His responsibilities were to clear log sawed timber.

Jim learned from working for Master Jenkins that there was another side to working in the woods; turpentine was an example. Before and following the antebellum period, the rural South's third-biggest employer was the naval store industry. Jim had over a third of his workers tapping the trees for sap. This was a tough job for slaves.

The blacksmith's shed was right next to the other hut. Jim wanted some of his slaves to begin with the rice fields. This work was exceedingly difficult because cleaning the land for cultivation usually meant claiming marshlands or swampy regions. One needed to construct dikes to hold freshwater and sluices to let it off. These dikes required considerable effort to build and maintain, in the company of snakes, alligators, and other vermin, using only picks, shovels, axes, and other hand tools. The male slaves had to plant, weed, and harvest in soggy, sickness-inducing fields. Then, towards the end of the year, planters adopted rice cultivation to the tide flow, allowing areas along certain rivers to be inundated with fresh water when the tides came in. The slaves' work was lessened at weeding time because flooding inhibited the growth of weeds, but the method required larger levees, sluices, and the building of canals between fields to carry off the crop. A lot of the men were sick with diseases transmitted by yellow fever-carrying mosquitos.

Jane liked Jean, the new cook, and showed her everything in the two kitchens. Jane wasn't going to be as formal as Master Jenkins was at dinner time, but she did enjoy eating in the dining room with her family and Joan. Jane and Jean cooked three meals a day for seventeen people. Jane took a food inventory every Monday; then, she and Jean would go into town and buy the food. They couldn't waste time as they had to be back in time to cook for everyone. It was five miles to town, and they left at six in the morning to buy their food and get around by ten.

They knew they had twenty dollars a week to spend on food to feed seventeen people. Jane purchased a sack of flour, pork, and cornmeal to make soup and stews for everyone. These dishes went a long way. Her one-pot meals combined meat, vegetables from their garden, and broth stretching out the meal proportions. Jane was aware that simmering meals over an open fire would feed a lot of people with cornbread. She also had maize, rice, peanuts, sweet potatoes from the garden, and dried beans for meals.

Jane and Jean got up every morning and worked in the garden before breakfast. They picked slap beans, dug up sweet potatoes, and picked onions, okra, and corn for the soup. Piles of sweet potatoes were cut for planting while the men hoed and plowed the earth. Jean carried the corn over to the corn husk where she removed all the corn off the cob into a large bowl. Jane went into the kitchen and sat down at the table. She cut up enough sweet potatoes and okra for the soup. Jane was very happy that she had indoor plumbing in the kitchen. She filled a large pan of water and placed the pan on the stove. She heated the water before dropping the meat and vegetables into the pot. After an hour, she stirred the soup, and the cornbread was baked in the oven at the same time. Pork had been the reigning delicacy in the South for a very long time, and Jane cooked it in everything she could.

Pork and ham were preserved. The meat is dried out with salt or, in some cases, pickled to store it safely for long periods. Jane preferred the taste of salted and smoked pork over pickled beef; plus, it was cheaper. While pork was the dominant food source, it was often served with corn at Jane's home. The primary ratio between her family and their slaves was typically an average of three pounds of pork per week. She purchased the lesser cuts of the hog, such as the feet, head, ribs, fatback, or internal organs. She hid the poor flavor of these cuts by marinating the meat with a powerful mixture of red pepper and vinegar.

Jane pulled the cornbread out of the oven. Cornbread was a delicious accompaniment to any meal, and it was particularly useful in soaking up every tasty morsel of sauce or juice of the soup or stew. Jane gave any leftover cornbread to the field hands for their lunches. Cornbread could be easily transported and could last a long time.

Jane remembered that when she was a child, the Master would feed all of the slaves at the big house because he kept them working from sunup to sundown. The slaves did not have any time to cook. Jim and Jane gave everyone an hour for lunch. This gave them time to eat, rest, and go back to work to do a better job.

Jane had Joan and Dora take the clothes, tablecloths, and bed covers to the wash house in baskets. Joan and Dora heated the water with soap in a cast-iron kettle. Once the wash was boiling, Joan took her wash stick and pounded it up and down to rotate the clothes to aerate the wash solution and loosen any dirt. Joan and Dora vigorously rubbed the clothes on a washboard until they were all clean.

As Dora was wringing out the items by hand, she looked at Joan and asked her, "Have you ever wanted to run away?"

"Sometimes," Joan told her before looking out the window and picking up a tablecloth to hang on the line to dry.

Dora lit the stove to heat her iron and set up her ironing board. Dora asked Joan, "Did you enjoy kissing Jack at the party?"

"It was very nice," Joan told her.

Jean and Jane were in the kitchen and needed to make butter. Jane showed Jean how to separate the milk into skim milk and cream; then, she poured the whole milk into a container and allowed the cream to rise to the top naturally.

"We will pour the milk into another container daily until several gallons accumulate. The cream will slightly sour due to the naturally occurring bacteria. This will increase the efficiency of the churning by using a butter churn. We will then take the butter out of the churn, wash it in very cold water, add salt, put the butter in small butter molds, and let it form the shape of the mold." Jane explained every step to her in detail so that the next time she would be able to do it herself.

Dora wanted to be a teacher. She talked to her parents about it. Jim told her she could use a room in the back, for an hour each day, to teach the slave children their A B C's. Paper was precious, so Dora wrote on the blackboard and had the children recite their lessons until they memorized them. Most of the time, Dora taught out of the Bible, a primer, and a hornbook. As the children grew older, their schooling prepared them for their adult roles on the plantation. Boys studied academic subjects, proper social etiquette, and plantation management, while girls learned English, math, reading, art, music, French, and the domestic skills suited to the mistress of a plantation. Dora enjoyed her classroom children and had a seat for every one of them. She was teaching them how to write, read, and do math. She knew these three things were important in life.

The mistress's role on a plantation consisted of many things. The smaller the plantation, the larger the role the woman took on because there were fewer slaves. Plantation mistresses were responsible for supervising all the slaves engaged in domestic plantation work and ensuring the smooth operation of domestic life. Jane had been doing more of this work in the kitchen and cleaning the plantation.

Women slaves like Jane quite literally got their hands dirty as they were washing, baking, ironing, nursing, and completing countless other domestic chores. Like Jane, they were in charge of deciding the meals for the day, making sure the household slaves were doing what they were supposed to, and, if necessary, helping her husband in the yard work.

CHAPTER TWENTY-ONE

THE MISTRESS OF THE HOME

Pam had a lot to do since she married Joe. One morning she woke up extremely sick and told Joe, "Please bring me a wet towel."

Joe looked at her, ran to the bathroom, hurried back, and placed the towel on her forehead. Pam asked him to help her into the bathroom as she felt sick. Joe was worried about her and helped her dress, and they headed to the doctor.

There was a doctor's office built just one mile from Joe's plantation. As Pam came out of the house, Joe picked her up and carried her to the carriage. She was as white as a ghost. Joe told Jerry to hurry and get to the doctor's office. Jerry looked at Pam, and with six children of his own, he just smiled. He knew what was wrong with Pam but didn't want to say anything.

Joe jumped out of the carriage and ran inside the doctor's office, and together they took Pam inside. Dr. Baker told Joe to wait in the waiting room and closed the door on him. Joe walked back and forth. He couldn't sit down as he was worried about Pam.

After about fifteen minutes, Dr. Baker came out smiling at Joe and told him, "You are going to be a dad." Wow!

Joe went into the examining room and helped Pam to the door and back into the carriage. Jerry already knew, but he waited for Joe to tell him.

Joe was holding Pam, "You are not to do anything when you get home. I will get you a slave nurse to do everything." Pam just looked up at him and smiled.

After a couple of months, Pam was feeling better and back to doing her chores at the plantation. Since she knew the plantation mistresses controlled the logistical side of the plantations, she understood better than most what the slaves needed. When slaves were sick, she made sure that food and clothing were available, and on special occasions such as weddings or funerals, she did her best to offer the necessary garments to slaves.

Pam loved to talk to the slave children and sit down by the river every morning and watch them play. She had Sue and Sally make cookies to hand out to them. Pam was aware the cooks shared their family recipes, and their food was always great.

Pam always listened to the slave's complaints. Sue informed her slave friend, "It is true, we have to approach the mansion door, with our hats in our hands, and subduing and beseeching language in our mouths - but, in return, we generally receive words of kindness from mistress Pam and very often a redress of our grievances" Sue told her, " I know very great ladies, who would never grant any request from the plantation hands, and sometimes Pam would refer them and their petitions to her husband, Joe."

Pam always used mild language with her slaves; often, they were sent to the overseer if she couldn't handle the problem. Everyone loved Pam and was excited about the pregnancy.

Pam called Sally into the office and told her she was going to town for food. She instructed her to bring her a list of the things they needed for the week.

Sally told her, "Yes, ma'am. I have the list right here," and she handed the list to Pam. Pam looked over the list and took it to Joe to get permission to buy the food on the list. Joe was okay with everything and wanted to know if she wanted him to go with her.

Pam told him, "No, I want to buy my cousin Judy something for her new baby girl, Lana Sue." Lana Sue was one month old now. Pam's dad had built her a baby bed and delivered the bed on the day she was born.

Pam was four months with a child now and was doing great. She told Joe she would take Sally with her if that was okay with him. Jerry brought the carriage around when Pam and Sally were ready to go. He helped Pam into the carriage, and Sally sat in the back seat. Jerry pulled up to a baby store in town and helped Pam and Sally out of the carriage.

Sally told Pam," I will wait here with Jerry. I can't wait to see what you get for Lana Sue."

Pam looked at many baby clothes and finally picked out two cute little dresses with bows and matching shoes. She asked the lady if she would wrap them in pretty paper and ribbon. Pam came out of the shop and told Sally all about the dresses; then, they went to the grocery store for food.

While the master controlled the plantation, the slave mistress was the administrator of domestic labor. While holding significantly less power than the master, slave mistresses were responsible for managing the household slaves. It was important to understand that although black and white women lived in the domestic sphere, their womanhood did not unite them.

Pam was aware that a mistress's main goal was a smooth-running household. That meant the mistress often supervised the training and assignments of slaves. A successful slave mistress had to control the slaves, often implementing violence. Pam's mother told her, "Protection is a luxury for white women with strings attached. To be protected, women need to obey a white man."

Jerry pulled up to the grocery store and helped first Pam and then Sally down from the carriage.

"I will be back soon," Pam said before walking into the store.

Sally had to stay outside with Jerry because no slaves were allowed inside. Pam gave the list to the store owner and strolled over to look at the fabric. She wanted a new dress as she was getting bigger. She had Joe's permission to purchase the material and instructed the store owner to give her two yards of fabric. The store owner boxed up the food and fabric and carried it outside for her where he handed it to Jerry. Jerry helped the ladies back into the carriage, loaded the food on the back, and rode home.

Southern women and Southern plantation mistresses were expected to portray the role of domestic housewife. Since they owned slaves, these women were free of manual labor or domestic duties and could focus on their children and husbands.

Pam was now nine months along and had started hurting at night. Joe had Pam's friend stay with them.

Joe ran and told May, "Pam needs you; I think the baby is on the way. I am going to fetch Doctor Baker. I will be back as quickly as I can." Joe jumped on Star, his horse, and rode through the night.

Dr. Baker was still up reading and told Joe, "I am right behind you, but it will be a while before your child comes into the world."

Joe didn't hear him as he was too busy jumping on his horse and riding back to his plantation.

Doctor Baker came into the house and instructed Joe to get him some hot water and bring it to him with towels. When Joe came to the bedroom door, May took the towels and water and told him to go back to the other room. Joe couldn't believe that he was told not to go into their bedroom. He was worried that Pam might need him!

After a few minutes, he heard Pam screaming, and Joe called up the stairs, " Did Pam have the baby?" He wondered what they were doing up there.

May yelled at him, "No."

Joe was trying to keep the annoyance out of his voice as he walked back and forth. After a few more minutes, Joe yelled to May, "Has the baby been born yet?"

May told him, "No! I have some time to straighten up. I'm just trying to make sure Pam doesn't have a mess to deal with right after the baby is born," May said as she came to the top of the stairs.

A few minutes later, the doctor delivered their son - John Ben Jenkins. May came down the stairs quickly and handed Joe a crying baby weighing five pounds. Joe stood there with a naked baby in a towel. As he looked down at his son John Ben, he asked May, "How's Pam?"

Pam called from the bedroom, "I am fine, Joe."

He tried to look past May but she pushed him back. "Let me get her cleaned up," May explained to Joe.

Joe looked down at his son nestled in the towel. Previously, he told Pam that he wanted to name their boy John. He didn't realize that she picked out a second name for the boy, Ben. He looked over at his son. He was born pale with black hair, blue eyes, ten fingers, and ten toes. Joe's son was looking up at him and Joe would have sworn that he smiled at him.

"Hey there, John Ben. I am your daddy." Joe rocked his son gently and then kissed him on the cheek. "It is so good to meet you finally."

May came out of Pam's room and allowed Joe and baby John Ben to enter the room. Pam was sitting up in bed, looking a bit pale and very tired. May had brushed her hair, and it was lying over her shoulders. Joe walked over with John Ben and laid him in her arms. Joe's eyes were still searching Pam's face, making sure Pam was fine. He leaned forward and kissed her on the lips. It still amazed him that he would be waking up next to this beautiful woman every day of his life. Pam stole his heart just two years earlier, and now he had his handsome son, John Ben

CHAPTER TWENTY-TWO

GOING TO CHURCH

Jane was told that there was a new church for black people in the area. She told Jim the night before they would all be going to the new church in the morning. The next morning, true to her word, Jane was up before the sun. She was coming in and out of the house as she prepared breakfast before they all left for church. Skippy, their faithful dog, followed quietly behind her on each trip. His face was down as though he knew he would be left behind.

Jane stood at the stove, scrambling eggs for their breakfast. She was used to rising while it was still dark. She never had time to sleep in long enough for the sun to wake her. Jim came into the house from the field, grabbed the coffee she poured him drinking it as he talked to her.

He set the cup down with a sigh. "I am going to get ready before I eat."

Jane scooped the eggs out of the pan and grabbed the pieces of toasted bread and crisp bacon. She placed their plates on the table. Joan and Dora had just come into the kitchen and sat down to eat. They were already dressed and wanted Jane to do their hair after breakfast.

"We will have to hurry with your hair so we won't be late. I still have to get ready," she told them.

Everyone enjoyed sitting at the long table in the dining room. Dora was reading about the possibility of a war.

"What does it say?" Jim asked.

Dora read out loud, "On November 6, Abraham Lincoln was elected President of the United States -- this event is outraging Southern states. The

Republican party has run on an anti-slavery platform, and many Southerners feel that there was long a place for them in the Union. As of December 20, South Carolina, Mississippi, Florida, Alabama, Georgia, Louisiana, and Texas have split from the Union."

Jim and Jane looked at each other as they listened.

Dora said, "The seceded states create the Confederate States of America and elect Jefferson Davis, a Mississippi Senator, as their provisional president."

Jim said, "This means a Civil War has begun."

Dora told them, "In here it says Lincoln proclaims that it was his duty to maintain the Union. He also declares that he has no intention of ending slavery where it exists or of repealing the Fugitive Slave Law -- a position that horrifies African Americans and their white allies."

Dora continued reading, "As of April 12, the Confederacy attacked Fort Sumter, a federal stronghold in Charleston, South Carolina. Federal troops returned the fire. "

Jane told them, "I am afraid this Civil War has begun."

Everyone started talking at once.

Jim told them, "Let's finish our breakfast as we have to get to church. I am sure we are going to hear a lot about the war at church."

Jim pulled the wagon up to the church and parked to the left. As he was helping Jane down, two of the men walked over to him and started talking to him about the war

"President Lincoln insists that the war is not about us or our rights; it is a war to preserve the Union," one of the men said.

"I read," another man said, "that most white northerners are not interested in fighting to free us slaves or in giving rights to us black people."

"I am going to be praying a lot. Friends, let's go inside before Jane comes looking for me," Jim said.

The past week had been busy and interesting. Jim and his family had just moved into their new home, and now they were going to the new church, just down the road. Dora was proud because she knew how to live here, and she was a good, gentle, and kind teacher. She hoped to talk to some of the parents to teach their children how to read and do math for one hour a day. Before, it would take her years to cram information into her head; now, she could learn the information in a matter of days.

The next Sunday, Joan told Jane, "I am not used to eating this early. At Jenkins Plantation, I usually stuff my pockets with bread and cheese in the morning and eat it when the sun is a bit higher in the sky. I would be in the fields at that time. I would sit under an oak tree and enjoy my treasures." She looked at Jane and told her, "Thanks for cooking."

Jane told her that she understood and placed the dirty pots into the sink basin. "I am going to have to wash these dishes when I come home from church."

Jane was glad she had found a church for the darkies. How many times had the Lord listened to and answered her prayers? Not always in the way she wanted, but God answered her prayers in his time. He had given them a beautiful home, their freedom, and now a lovely church. She smiled as she walked with her family to church. She knew everything was going to be alright if God had anything to do with it.

When they approached the church, Dora watched several families with children laughing, talking, and walking up the steps entering the building. Some dressed like her, others more of a version of the latest fashion, and others dressed in clothing far more worn. But all in all, everyone seemed happy to be there.

Dora looked up at her mama and asked, "Is this here our church?"

Jane looked over at her daughter and told her, "Yes, it is. It's a Negro town, Dora. Everything you see around here is owned by us Negro's. See Dora, it ain't gonna be so bad, here in our new town."

Dora was glad to hear it, and she hoped the parents would love for her to teach their children. Jane had told them the town was run by Negroes, but it is one thing to hear that and another to believe it!

Jim escorted his family into the church just as the first song started. As everyone found a seat, they picked up a songbook and joined in singing,

"The Old Rugged Cross". Everything about the church was genuinely nice. It wasn't like the white people's church! This church had clear and bright, clean windows, a beautiful, clean, and smooth wood floor, and new and shiny pews.

Dora and Joan whispered to each other, "Now it is only the reverend that can preach." Both wanted to come back every Sunday.

Joan noticed that the wife of a man in front of her was about to have a baby, and it looked like it was due any minute. The woman smiled and gave Joan a small wave. Both Joan and Dora returned the wave. Jane elbowed Dora in excitement, indicating that they were now making friends. Dora wanted to teach, and Joan could sew clothes and help deliver a few babies.

They sang several songs, and then a young man made a few announcements, He then announced that the Shell family had just moved to town and had also joined the church. He told everyone there was going to be a potluck tonight at five and could everyone please be sure to bring something.

His next announcement was that the women were getting a sewing group together starting Saturday for all of the young ladies that wanted to learn to sew. Jane, Joan, and Dora wanted to go to both the dinner and the sewing group.

The preacher walked up to his stand and looked out in the crowd." I know most of you here today have been told or read about the war we are about to have and about how the government is turning away our boys' volunteers that are rushing to enlist. Lincoln upholds the laws barring blacks from enlisting in the army, proving to northern whites that their racial privilege will not be threatened. I am told there are exceptions. However, we black Americans have been working aboard naval vessels for years, and there is no reason to continue. I read this morning that because of this our black sailors will be accepted into the U.S. Navy from the beginning of the war."

Some of the younger men praised the Lord.

The preacher said, "We know Lincoln is not ready to admit it, but us Blacks know that this is a war against slavery. During the so-called era of the Indian Wars in the west, roughly fourteen thousand African American men served in the segregated infantry and cavalry units in the Great Plains and the Rocky Mountains. I heard the Indians called us 'the Buffalo Soldiers.' I have also been told the CCC employs some two hundred thousand young black men out of work to carry out much-needed conservation work on national forests and other public lands. Although the law specifically bans racial discrimination, some of you may want to join the CCC. I have been told African American men will not be sent out of their home states. Black camps will not be forced on local communities, and Black people will not be selected according to economic need, even though they are often in much more dire economic conditions than their white counterparts. Let us pray. I am praying for all of our boys this morning, black and white Lord, that you will see somehow have a better way to settle this, in Jesus's name amen!"

The offering plate was passed around, and Jim put a few coins in. Joan didn't have any money. She wanted her own money, she realized, as she sat there. She wanted a job and to never have to depend on a man. She was tired of the way whites were treating the blacks.

Jane noticed that the reverend was a young man. More than that, the girls said he was handsome."

"For those of you who have Bibles, let's turn to the book of Luke," the reverend said with his deep, calm, and soothing voice

Both Joan and Dora asked Jane. "What is his name?"

Jane looked at them and smiled, "Reverend Peter Russell."

Reverend Peter Russell presented his message in a truly kind and clear way showing he knew his Bible and had been watching other preachers. He didn't do a lot of shouting as some preachers did on the stage, but he got his sermon across. Dora and Joan listened to everything he said and were excited for more. After an hour, they were back on their feet for the last song of the service. They looked around the church again, noticing the families and the happy children talking on the way out of the church door.

As they started out of the pew, Reverend Russell came up to them and told them he was glad they came today, and to be sure and come back tonight to the potluck dinner.

Jane told him they would be at the potluck for sure and would bring some fried chicken." As Jane walked out of the church and down the steps, she inhaled deeply. She hadn't cried in years, but she had found Jesus this morning. That was something she hadn't had in a long time. She felt like she was having the best day of her life as she walked with her family home.

Jane walked into the kitchen and put her apron over her dress. She told Jim to go out into the yard and kill six of her chickens, clean them, and bring them in to cook. Today was Sunday, and all the slaves had the day off and cooked for themselves. Jane was going to cook two chickens for her family and take the rest to church that night.

She asked Dora, "Can you cut up potatoes to mash? Joan, can you make biscuits and gravy?"

Dora grabbed enough potatoes and started peeling them, while Joan grabbed enough flour for the biscuit batter. The family loved to sit around the big table and talk about their week.

Jim was reading the paper while sitting at the table after dinner. He was reading about how the election of Mr. Lincoln was received in the South in Virginia. He read out loud. "The great national or sectional, battle has been fought, and although the official report of it has not been completed, there can be no manner of doubt that victory has perched upon the Black Republican banner. The issue has been disastrous to the Union cause. The triumph of sectionalism has laid the foundation for all the mischief and ills to the country that was predicted and deprecated by Washington Farewell Address. It is a gloomy exercise of the mind to contemplate the new aspect of things, but the people must look at it and ponder it."

"It is time now for the wisest hands and most patriotic hearts in the land to enlist in the great work of adjusting matters in such a way as to save the Republic, if possible, from the almost certain perdition which stares it in the face."

Jim was excited as he read on. "Lincoln wins: After the historic debates with Lincoln, Stephen Douglas found himself vilified by Southern Democrats. He tried unsuccessfully to argue that his way would enable the nation to pass over the momentary issue of slavery in the territories and thus preserve the Union. But Southern radicals would have none of it. When the Democratic convention met in Charleston, nominations enabled Southern Democrats to veto South Carolina, on April 23, both Northern and Southern delegates were ready for a showdown. The first test came when the Southern delegates insisted on a plank favoring a federal slave code for the territories. Knowing that he would lose every Northern state if he agreed, Douglas refused to endorse the plank. When the delegates defeated the plank by a small majority, fifty Southern delegates, led by Alabama "fire-eater," walked out of the convention."

"The amazing fact about the election is that it occurred in the first place. In the middle of a devastating civil war, the United States held its presidential election almost without discussing any alternatives. No other democratic nation had ever conducted a national election during times of war. And while there was some talk of postponing the election, it was never given serious consideration, even when Lincoln thought he would lose. Lincoln won with a popular vote of fifty-five percent."

Jim looked at his family and told them, "I am afraid we are going to have a big war on our hands."

opinion will overwhelmingly back the North. We can't let this happen, my friends. Let's get to work!"

As Joe rode Star home, he felt that it was the beginning of the end of slavery, and he was going to have to pay the slaves for their work. He and the other men feared that Lincoln would give in to pressure from Northern conservatives and would fail to keep his promise. At the meeting, all the men agreed with Joe.

Before he left the hotel Joe told them, "Please come back here tomorrow night at five with your list."

After a lot of deliberating and praying Joe stopped to eat a quick lunch and read about the Battle of Black Jack in one of the papers he purchased. Joe realized that he could no longer afford to bury his head in the sand and hope that everyone and everything was going to be alright. He had to get all the business bought before someone else did it for him.

When Joe got home, he sat at his desk. He knew steel and oil were big businesses. Also, The North and the South would require a steamboat. The South would need these three items. Joe planned to start buying up all the steel and oil companies he could. He told his friends to start buying every steamboat on the rivers. With the introduction of such new technology as the Bessemer converter and the open-hearth process, the amount of steel produced in the United States went from seventy-seven thousand tons in 1870 to over ten million tons in 1900. Joe was glad he was a part of this. Joe acquired other steel companies that were unable to compete with his highly efficient operations. He also bought iron ore deposits, steamships, and railroad cars. These railroad cars were used to ship his ore to his plants and goods to his customers.

The president remained firm despite fierce opposition. He issued the final Emancipation Proclamation; this document officially freed all slaves within the states or parts of states in rebellion and not in Union hands. This resulted in one million slaves in Union territory still in bondage.

Throughout the North, African Americans and their White allies were exuberant. They packed churches and meeting halls to celebrate the news.

In the South, most slaves did not hear of the proclamation for months. The Civil War had not changed anything. The North was not only fighting to preserve the Union, but it was fighting to end slavery. Joe and his friends were ready for it!

Slavery was the cornerstone of the Confederacy, and cotton was its foundation. Joe purchased all the cotton he could find. Cotton also spawned a series of federal regulations during the war. He knew the North required cotton for its textile mills, and it wanted to deprive the South of its financing power. Joe obtained a permit from the Treasury Department to purchase cotton in the Confederate states. He planned to buy cotton for as little as twelve cents a pound, transport it to New York on his ship lines for three cents a pound, and sell it for 1.98 a pound and make a great profit. Joe and his plantation friends kept slaves in the cotton fields working sixteen hours a day, seven days a week. Blacks were denied economic and physical mobility by federal government policy. That was due to the racial animosity of Northern Whites and the enduring need for cotton labor in the South. The federal government was forced to confront what to do with slave refugees and those who escaped behind Union lines.

Joe and his friends decided free slaves would be in the military service or work on the abandoned cotton plantations to till the ground. Former slaves were contracted to work on the abandoned plantations around Vicksburg, Mississippi. Joe paid each slave ten dollars a month, and they worked ten hours a day. Joe didn't let the slaves or his family leave the plantation without a pass. He also worked with many slave men and women on his steamboats, ships, and loading docks.

Throughout this time, Northern Black men continued to pressure the army to enlist them. A few individual commanders in the field took steps to recruit Southern African Americans into their forces. But it was only after Lincoln issued the Final Emancipation Proclamation that the federal army officially accepted Black soldiers into its ranks.

African American men rushed to enlist everywhere there was an enlisting station. This time they were accepted into all-black units. By the end of the war, more than one hundred and eighty-six thousand Black soldiers had joined the Union army; ninety-three thousand from the Confederate states, forty thousand from the border slave states, and fifty-three thousand from the free states. Black soldiers faced discrimination as well as segregation. The army was extremely reluctant to commission Black officers -- only one hundred gained commissions during the war. The Black soldiers were also given substandard supplies and rations. The worst form of discrimination was probably the pay differential. They often wrote home to their families, telling them how bad it was for them.

At first, the back enlistment assumed that Blacks will not engage in direct combat, and the men are paid as laborers rather than as soldiers. Black soldiers, therefore, received $7 per month, plus a $3 clothing allowance; in contrast, white soldiers received $13 per month, plus 3.50 for clothes.

On January 1, 1863, resident Abraham Lincoln signed the Emancipation Proclamation: "All persons held as slaves within any States in rebellion against the United States," it declared, "shall be then, thenceforward, and forever free."

After the Civil War broke out, abolitionists such as Douglas argued that the enlistment of Black soldiers would help the North win the war and would be a huge step in the fight for equal rights: "Once you let the Black man get upon his person, the brass letters, U.S.; let him get an eagle on his button, and a musket on his shoulder and bullets in his pocket," Douglas said, " there is no power on earth which can deny that he has earned the right to citizenship." President Lincoln was afraid of this because escaped slaves would push the loyal border states to secede.

CHAPTER TWENTY-FOUR

FRIDAY NIGHT DANCES

Friday morning, the sun was coming through the window as Dora lay there dreaming of the dance and her date with Paul tonight. She had met Paul at church on Sunday and thought he was the most handsome man in the world. She couldn't believe it when he asked her to attend the dance with her.

Dora crawled out of bed and headed to the water pitcher. June brought warm water and a towel to Dora's room. Dora loved waking up in the morning to warm water. She enjoyed having someone bring her warm water; it was the norm for her now that she lived in the big house. She picked up the pitcher and poured the warm water into a large white bowl sitting on her dresser. She smiled at her reflection in the mirror.

Just as Dora finished washing her face, Joan knocked on her door. Dora was excited to see her and told her, "Come on in and I will try my dress on." Dora pulled the dress out of the chifforobe and danced around the room, holding it up to her.

Joan smiled at her, "Let's try on everything!"

Joan helped her put on the chemise, then the case and corset. After that, the two tiers of petticoats gave her an extra grown-up lift. Joan called June into the room to help her put Dora's dress over her head and smooth out all the wrinkles. Dora looked beautiful. Joan put Dora's flat shoes on her and instructed her to turn around so she could fix anything that needed fixing. Joan didn't see anything wrong with Dora's lovely dress. Dora was going to be the best-looking girl at the dance.

Joan told Dora to sit down in front of the mirror, and she would braid her hair and fix the braids on top of her head with ribbons coming down her back.

Paul couldn't wait to see Dora again. He was wearing a plain green shirt with blue jeans, a cowboy hat, and black boots. Paul instructed his buttler Joey to bring his horse and wagon around. He was almost ready to go. He had bought Dora a flower to match her dress.

Joey brought the wagon around, and Paul stepped up into it placing the box with Dora's flower on the seat beside him. Paul rode down the road five miles to Dora's parents' home and stopped in front. He walked to the front door and knocked. Jim opened the door and shook Paul's hand. He told him to come in and have a seat and he would go up and get Dora. Paul walked over to the living room and waited for Dora's dad to bring her down.

Jim knocked on Dora's door and told her that Paul was downstairs waiting for her. Dora looked breathtaking as she walked down the stairs. Her dad put out his arm for Dora and walked her down the stairs.

Paul stood up as she came down the stairs. He couldn't believe she could look more beautiful than she had on Sunday. As Dora stepped off the last step, Paul took her arm and pinned her flower on her shoulder.

Dora told him, "I love the flowers. Thank you. You look very handsome, Paul."

Paul opened the door and escorted Dora out the door and down the front steps to the wagon. Dora lifted her dress in the front, and Paul helped her into the wagon and then went around to the other side and climbed up into the seat beside her. He looked at Dora and told her how beautiful she looked. Paul picked up the reins and headed down the drive to the barn dance a mile away. As he looked at Dora, he wished it were ten miles.

As they rode to the dance the sun was just beginning to set. It was a mellow golden color and soaked up the atmosphere as they rode by the lake. Paul and Dora pulled up in front of the barn, and Paul pulled the wagon to the right.

As Paul helped her down he said, " Let's go have a great time." He took Dora's arm, walked her to the open door, pulled out thirty cents, and paid for the dance.

Paul walked Dora over to a hay bale where Dora sat down. "Would you like some punch?" He asked.

Paul hurried to get Dora her punch, he couldn't wait to get back to her. He didn't want any other man asking her to dance. When he returned with her drink he sat down beside her.

Dora had never been to a barn dance before, and she asked Paul, "Please tell me about the barn dance."

Paul explained to her, "A wooden floor is made for dancing and replaces the dirt floor in this large riding arena of the barn. They decorate with hay bales for sitting and Italian lights overhead to have just the right touches to recreate old dances of yesteryear. If you want to take a break or just listen as the music drifts in the night air, we can sit around the large bonfire blazing outside the barn entrance. It is a lot of fun putting marshmallows on a stick, toasting and blowing them out, and eating them while still hot. We can walk outside later for this when it gets cooler."

Dora loved everything about the decorations of the barn. Bales of hay were placed all around for everyone to sit on. A wagon with hay was in one corner with a saddle across the wheel and a wood barrel in front. On stage were wagon wheels, hay, and guitars. In another corner was a covered wagon with the side cover rolled up with more bales of hay for sitting. Lanterns blazed all around the barn.

Paul asked Dora, "Would you like to square dance? I will show you how."

"I would love it. It looks like fun."

Paul stood up, looked down at Dora, took her hand, and walked out to the dance floor. "Everyone makes mistake. If you bump into someone just smile and say sorry." He looked down into Dora's eyes, "Just think about getting to the right place for the next move on time."

The caller on the stage told everyone to get a girl and come and join in the fun! "We are going to Square Dance the night away!"

Everyone who wanted to dance joined Paul and Dora in the middle of the dance floor. The band started playing, and the caller began the dance. "Let's begin! Get yourself a partner and jump right in! Right hand! Left hand! Around you go! Now back-to-back your partner in a do-si-do. Now, move to the center for a curtsy and a bow!"

Dora was all over the place but having a lot of fun. It was lively and free. The banjo, fiddle, and guitar people were all playing at the same time.

The caller called out the next moves. "Forward up and back; take three steps to your partner, bow and curtsy, and take three steps back. Next, right elbow swing; in eight counts, step forward, hook right elbows with your partner, go around on time, then let go of the elbows and keep it on time." Then he called, "Left elbow swing; same as the right, next two hand swing through the night; step forward and join both hands, moving clockwise, go around the circle one more time. Go back to your place then do-si-do while facing the same direction as you go, make a circle around your partner, pressing your right shoulders first back-to-back and then left shoulders and back, now you got the knack. Back to starting place."

"Next, head couples-sashay down; have a good time and don't you frown. Couple at the end or top step forward. join your hands out to the sides and then slide down the center for eight counts while the others stomp and clap. Then sashay back; the same head couple slides back the other way shuffles eight counts and ends up back where they started.

Dora and Paul were having a great time and were laughing as they walked off the floor. Dora told him, "I have never had such a good time in all my life."

"We will dance slow the next time," Paul said as he laughed with her.

At ten, Paul and Dora were ready to leave. Paul took Dora's hand and walked her out to the wagon before he helped her up inside. He leaned down and kissed her on the lips. Dora kissed him back somehow knowing she wanted to live the rest of her life with this man.

CHAPTER TWENTY-FIVE

DORA MEETS PAUL'S SISTER

Paul looked at Dora and grinned. He couldn't think of another woman that could pass muster when he compared them to the breathtaking beauty of Dora Shell. No other woman got his blood moving the way Dora did. It was time to ask this woman about marriage.

Paul had decided that it was time for Dora to meet his family. They were on their way to meet his sister, Betsy. Paul knew in his heart that he wanted to make Dora his wife. He turned the wagon in the direction of his sister's home.

Coming down the road paul pointed at a two-story house and said, "That is my sister's home, Dora,"

They passed several homes on their way to Betsy's home, and Dora thought all the houses were lovely. Betsy's home was set away from the road. Going up to the house was a brick path with small bushes on either side leading to the front steps. She had a lovely long front porch with two rockers on each side of the door. Directly above the porch was a balcony.

Dora could see there was also a rather large porch on the right side of the house. The first floor had four large windows with black shutters. The story above it was the same. Behind the house, she could see a small barn and a shed with hay. It was a beautiful home, the likes of which she could have never imagined being owned by anyone.

Dora asked him, "Is your sister married?"

"Yes, ma'am," he smiled as he looked over at her.

As Dora looked at Betsy's home, she liked everything she saw. Paul stopped at the end of the road while Dora looked at Paul's sister's home. Dora saw a woman come out of the house.

Paul's sister asked Paul, "Are you going to sit at the end of the road all day or come see me? My children keep peering out the windows, wondering why you haven't moved in the past ten minutes?"

"Betsy," Paul said, "I brought Dora with me to meet you."

Paul's horse clipped-clopped down the road toward his sister's home. Betsy lifted her skirt, walked down the steps then down the brick pathway. Betsy was so excited to see Paul, and she was glad he had Dora with him.

Dora thought Paul's sister was stunning. She was tall, had a light brown complexion, dark curly hair that was pinned up on her head, and had large brown eyes. She had a small and delicate figure and looked to be about thirty years old.

"Hello," she called out to Dora as they got closer. Dora slowly stepped out of the wagon with Paul's help and met Betsy halfway.

"Hi, Betsy," Dora said when just a foot separated them.

Betsy held out her hand and told Dora to come on into her home.

Betsy had two boys and a girl. As Dora looked past her she saw the children come down the steps of the house, walking toward them. One little boy was wearing brown breeches, a white shirt, and a royal blue vest. He took long strides on his way to see them. His hair touched the back of his shirt and was parted to the side. He had a light-color skin tone, like his mother's.

Betsy put her arm around her son and introduced Dora to her children, "This is Ben, Danny, and Sally," she said as they all ran toward Paul and gave him a big hug.

"Come on in, I was just putting dinner on the table." Betsy told, Dora "Let me show you where to freshen up."

As Dora walked into the bathroom she observed that the floors were marble, the tub was massive, the soap was rose-scented, and the water was piping hot. She didn't want to leave, but she knew everyone was waiting on her in the dining room. She grabbed the fluffy white towel on the nearest counter and dried off quickly as she looked in the mirror to check her hair and makeup. Dora looked at her reflection, and she was happy with what she saw. She walked over to the door and took a deep breath. She was a bit nervous as she walked to the dining room.

Betsy's husband had come home for dinner. As Dora walked into the dining room, Bob stood up and came around to Dora, took her hand, and told her, "I am Bob. We are so glad Paul brought you with him. Please, have a seat," he said as he pulled her a chair out.

Paul's parents, Ed and Linda, lived about a mile behind the bank that Bob owned. Bob had everyone hold hands and pray. "Father, thank you for this great day, thank you for this meal you have given us, and thank you for Paul and Dora. In Christ's name, Amen."

The children started passing the food around the table, talking and laughing all at the same time. Dora began to relax and joined in with them. After dinner, Bob told the children to clean the table, and the adults walked out to the backyard. There was an extensive, fenced-in garden with all kinds of vegetables. Betsy used a lot of herbs for medicinal purposes and grew a lot of produce for both eating and selling. Dora watched as the children moved slowly up and down the different rows picking the vegetables and putting them in baskets.

Betsy told Dora, "Our children are particularly good with the garden. They hoe every day keeping the weeds and grasses out."

Sally ran over to Dora to show her the tomatoes she just picked. Dora reached down and hugged her, and told her, "They are so big and pretty. "

Sally smiled up at her and said, "Yes, ma'am, they are."

The children picked up all the baskets, carried them to the kitchen, and poured them into the sink. Sally turned on the water and filled the sink.

Betsy and Dora walked through the back door into the kitchen. Dora asked her, "Would you like for me to help you with the vegetables,"

"No, they like to do it. Let's go into the living room, sit down, and relax and talk," Betsy told her.

Dora told Betsy all about her being a slave and how her mom and dad inherited an estate home from her great-uncle.

Betsy talked about Paul, her husband, and her children. Betsy mentioned that she was getting a sewing club together. "Would you like to join us, Dora?"

Dora explained to her that she taught children to read and write on Mondays and Tuesdays. "But outside of that, I can sew with you. One of the ladies that lives with us sews, and I can see if she would like to come with me."

Betsy told her, "That sounds great. I look forward to seeing you both at the sewing club."

When they got back to Dora's home, Paul stopped the horse, helped her down from the wagon, and kissed her good night. She told him she had a wonderful time with his family.

When Dora got into the house she headed straight for Joan's room. She wanted to tell her all about her day with Paul and how she met his sister and his family.

She told Joan, "Betsy is having a sewing club and wanted you and I to attend. What do you think? "

"I would love to attend the sewing club with you. I can go Wednesday and Thursday."

Wednesday at 1:00, Joan, Jane, and Dora pulled the wagon up to Betsy's home. Three more wagons were already there. All three ladies were excited as they stepped down from the wagon and walked up to the front door. Betsy had told them to bring several pieces of fabric in red, white, and blue, a needle, and thread; they were making a flag quilt.

Betsy answered the door and greeted them with, "Happy Wednesday, sweet friends. Our Mississippi weather is so nice today. It is one of those days we can open our windows without freezing. It is nice to hear the birds singing today. Betsy introduced everyone and instructed all the ladies to have a seat behind a sewing machine.

As the ladies sat behind a sewing machine, Betsy began speaking to them about the flag quilt. "I have a flag quilt I have made, and many people asked me about the pattern I used. I made my blocks smaller. I will share my measurements with all of you. Then, you all can start making a flag quilt." All the ladies were excited about the project. They started getting out their fabric and supplies. "Does anyone need scissors," Betsy asked, but everyone had their own.

"I need everyone to go over to the cutting table and spread out your fabric to be cut. I will give you a valuable tip. I like to cut my strips a tad bit longer for squaring up. Betsy then gave all the women the measurements for all the squares they needed. She gave them time to cut the material before giving them directions on how to sew them.

"If you need help, just let me know, we have all the time we need… this year." Some of the ladies were new sewers and needed more time to learn; that is why Betsy wanted to start a sewing class.

At the end of the class, Betsy told them, "Ladies, just leave everything where it is, and you can continue tomorrow." The ladies all had a great time and when they stood up to get their purses they all hugged Betsy. They all echoed how much they appreciated her teaching them.

Everyone came back Thursday to the sewing class, and Betsy had them finish what they had been working on before starting the next class with everyone. Betsy showed them her work. Some ladies had a hard time, and the measurements were off, but Betsy told them, "It is ok. You will get better as you learn." Betsy helped them learn and showed them how it was supposed to look.

As the ladies worked, Betsy told them, "Next week, we will sew the top to the back and put in cotton in the middle. Then we will hand sew it down. I hope all of you get to do something you love today."

At the end of the class, she instructed them to just leave the work on their machines again and that they would work on it next Wednesday. She then thanked them all for coming. The ladies all talked as they gathered their things and got up to leave and go home.

Two days later, Paul picked up Dora to go to the cafe for breakfast. They requested a table at the front corner by the window. Paul sat with his back to the wall; he was able to look out the window and watch people as they passed by. Paul told Dora about his neighbor getting stuck in the window of his house trying to climb back in after being in town all night. Dora laughed about it as she sipped her coffee.

Paul told her, "The sheriff had to grease him down like a pig to get him out of the hole in the window area."

"Why is he sneaking back into the house?" Doa asked.

Paul laughed and told her, "He doesn't want Betty Lou to know he was in town drinking or gambling or whatever he was doing in that place."

Dora told him all about his sister's sewing class and what a great time she had. She elaborated on the little squares she had cut out and tried to sew them together. "I hope I can get better, right now I am hopeless."

The waitress came over and told them, "The special for today is country ham with red-eye gravy and grits. We also have a pan of cinnamon rolls that just came out of the oven."

Paul told the waitress, "We will both have the specials and the roll. I am hungry. Bring some more coffee too please."

Dora smiled at Paul's comments, "What if I didn't want a roll?"

Paul took her hand and said, "I will eat it too."

When the cinnamon rolls were brought to the table, Dora couldn't help herself. She gobbled her cinnamon roll and even took a bite of Paul's. They were delicious.

Paul was still holding her hand when he asked, "I'm curious, what do you think about getting married? "Dora looked at him in surprise! Paul waited until she came back to earth before he spoke again. Paul told her, "I love you, and you are the most beautiful woman I have ever laid eyes on. I want to spend the rest of my life with you." Paul reached into his pocket and pulled out a beautiful ring with three diamonds, and waited for her answer.

Dora couldn't believe it. She loved Paul, and her answer was, "Yes. Oh, Yes, always yes."

Paul took the ring out of the box, placed the ring on her finger, and sealed it with a kiss. Paul helped Dora up and left a tip for the waitress. On the way home, Paul pulled over to the side of the road and kissed her softly on her lips.

When he got Dora home Paul told her, "I will see you soon. I have a lot of work to do this morning." Paul owned a railroad company. Before Paul left he asked her, "Do you know anyone good with figures? I need people to work at the office for me."

Dora told him that she would think about it. Dora enjoyed teaching two days a week, but she had taken business classes in college and was particularly good at math. When she got in the house she headed straight to the kitchen where Jane and Joan were busy cutting up potatoes. Dora was all smiles when she entered the kitchen.

As she entered the kitchen she said, "I am getting married." She showed the ladies her beautiful ring. Jane and Joan were excited for her and gave her a big hug.

They had a lot to talk about around the kitchen table that day. Dora told them all about her breakfast with Paul and how he asked her to marry him."He wants to know if I know anyone that wants to work in his office." Dora said, " I think I would like to work Wednesday, Thursday, and Friday for him. That way, I can teach the children Monday and Tuesday."

The next weekend when Paul came by to see Dora, she told him that she would like to work in the office with him.

"I will come to pick you up Wednesday morning and take you to the office after we get a bite to eat," Paul said excitedly.

Wednesday morning, Dora was wearing a blue dress with a matching hat. Paul arrived at about eight, and together they headed into town for breakfast. Paul went over everything she would be doing as they ate their sweet rolls.

CHAPTER TWENTY-SIX

WORKING FOR THE RAILROAD

The town of Crowley was growing in leaps and bounds. There was a school, church, bank, lawyer's office, livery stable, four stores, and Paul's office for the railroads right by the train track and river. During the American Civil war, many armies relied heavily on railroads and steamboats to bring in supplies for the Confederate States Army. The system was fragile and was ideal for short hauls of cotton to the nearest river or ocean port.

During the war, new parts were hard to obtain, and Dora's job was to get parts where they needed to go. Some railroads lost their main source of income with the cotton crop being hoarded under the "King Cotton" theory. Paul knew many employers had to lay off employees and even let go of their skilled technicians and engineers.

Dora was very excited about her new job. There were two desks in the front office and through another door was Paul's office. Paul spent a few hours going over everything she would be doing, from filing to answering the telephone.

Paul told her, "We run trains all over the U.S.A. The Confederacy has just built a five and a half miles spur off the Orange and Alexandria Railroad at Manassas Junction toward Centreville, Virginia, known as the Centreville Military Railroad."

"We are sending supplies necessitated by the Confederacy's small industrial base. They need us to transport engines and cars to them. The department orders all the passenger trains to give governmental trains the right of way to get supplies through. We are on the verge of collapse. I don't want to see this. I need your help in every way possible."

Paul and Dora were run ragged for the next year. Feeders were being scrapped for replacement steel for railroad lines, and the continual use of rolling stock wore them down faster than they could be replaced.

Paul knew Joe Jenkins owned the steamships, and they were working together to get supplies to different places. Paul, Joe, and Dora were always having meetings about what to do. The Union armies pushed further into Confederate territory, and they had former Confederate railway lines or what was left of them. Confederate troops generally applied a scorched-earth policy toward railroads when they were retreating. Union troops often had to rebuild an entire line from scratch for it to be usable, and that is where the trains and steamships become useful and got the supplies to different areas.

Paul's office ordered supplies from Joe. Due to the vagaries of the war, some lines would be rebuilt six or seven times by differing sides, especially in states like Virginia, where fighting was most intense. Dora made sure to keep all the orders up to date and made sure they were delivered on time.

Every day attempts were made to enlarge the Confederacy's rail system by adding or connecting lines. Of the three major rail projects the Confederate congress proposed and funded, only one of them was a connection between Danville, Virginia, and Greensboro, North Carolina. Joe and Paul weren't happy about that.

The army foraged liberally in the country during the march. Under the command of discreet officers, foraging parties were organized. They gathered corn, any kind of meat, vegetables, or whatever the command needed. They aimed to keep at least ten days' provisions. Soldiers would not trespass on the property or enter the dwellings of the inhabitants. Yet during a halt or a camp, they gathered turnips, apples, and other vegetables from the fields and drove animals to their camp.

People were losing food in their fields and started fighting back. The army corps commanders were entrusted with the power to destroy mills, houses, and cotton gins, and people were left without anywhere to live. They were burning bridges, obstructing roads, and manifesting local hostility. They took all the horses, mules, and wagons. "War was no game."

The importance of rivers in this landscape could not be overstated. These swift-running trains afforded the controlling army huge strategic advantages. They could quickly transport soldiers to any point that bordered a controlled track or waterway with steamboats. But the army had to be careful. Any army that advanced overland with an enemy-controlled river on its flank was in the perpetual crippling danger of a surprise attack from the rear of the boat.

The rivers were also vital arteries for the Confederate economy, although lines of trade and communication were easily severed by patrolling enemy gunboats. Paul and Joe were aware of this issue as it was becoming especially apparent as the Union navy took control of longer and longer swathes of the Mississippi River.

As Paul and Joe worked hard sending supplies down the river, the Civil War began with both sides scrambling to put their navy on a war footing. Dora was aware that the Federal navy outnumbered its Southern counterpart. Joe knew that neither side had enough combat-capable warships at the onset of the struggle. Joe, Paul, and Dora worked day and night, keeping the trains and boats running.

In the summer of 1863, the fall of Vicksburg brought Mississippi entirely under Union control and split the Confederacy in half. Union forces used their increasing control of the waterways to concentrate more and more strength at decisive points. At the same time, Southern armies could barely risk an advance with exposed waterways in their rear.

After the spring of 1862, when the Confederates lost Fort Henry, Fort Donaldson, Memphis, Tennessee, and New Orleans in Louisiana, Vicksburg became the key remaining point of their defense on the Mississippi River. The capture of Vicksburg yielded the North's control of the river and thus enabled it to isolate those Confederate states that lay west of the river from those in the east. Joe and Paul saw Vicksburg as ideally suited for defensive purposes. However: it was located on high bluffs along the river and was protected on the north by a maze of swampy bayous.

Grant moved his army of forty thousand troops to the west bank of the Mississippi. He marched south along the river for a considerable distance until he could recross the river at Bruinsburg crossing, which lay about thirty miles south of Vicksburg. His army recrossed to the east bank of the river using a Union fleet.

At one of Paul's trains in Newton's Station, Mississippi, Union cavalry raiders under the command of Col. Benjamin Grierson, disrupted Confederate communications, probed deep into enemy territory, and entered the town of Newton's Station. They succeeded in securing the town without any serious fighting and captured two of Paul's Confederate trains.

Paul called Dora into his office, "They just destroyed two of our trains, several miles of railroad track, and telegraph wires. I can't get through to see how bad it is. Please send a wire to Joe and tell him to get down here fast."

"We had a passenger on one of those trains, ammunition, and whiskey. They have burned down half of the town, our uniforms and arms building. Our railroad depot was burned, but the hospital staff did get out the medicine and food."

Paul told Dora, "Go collect a train of one hundred wagons and send them to Vicksburg and load them with rations. See if you can get one hundred thousand pounds of bacon, the balance of coffee, sugar, salt, and hard bread. I don't have to remind you of the overwhelming importance of celerity in your movements. The road to Vicksburg is open. All we want now are men, ammunition, and hard bread." Dora quickly wired all these requests to different places and had it done in no time.

Joe was losing badly. He had to call a meeting and figure out what to do. Ultimately, the South's static defense on the rivers couldn't contend with the irresistible mobile offense execution with such skill by officers such as Foote, Grant, and Farragut. In a military and economic sense, the loss of the inland arteries had all but dismembered the Confederacy.

Vicksburg was one of the Union Army's most successful campaigns of the American Civil War. The Vicksburg campaign was also one of the longest.

Joe's steamboat, Sand City, carried a crew of ninety-five. For two years, she ran a regular route between St. Louis and New Orleans and was frequently commissioned to carry troops. However, the capacity of the Sand City was only three hundred and seventy-six passengers. Joe had the steamboat built for speed and capacity. The vessel measured two hundred and sixty feet long was thirty-nine feet wide at the base, forty-two feet wide at the beam, displaced seven hundred and nineteen tons and drew just seven feet of water.

The steamboat had seventy cabins and deck passengers and a small amount of livestock with loads and loads of cotton and supplies. Joe Jenkins had eight steamboats he used to travel. They carried people and goods from one place to another, and Dora kept up with all of it. Dora had over fifty wagons without wheels on one steamboat. The wheels were coming on the next boat. River travel was often slow as it depended on the river currents, wind, and manpower.

One day Joe came into Paul's office and told him, "I got great news. We must invest in steam-powered boats. They will travel at an astonishing speed of up to five miles per hour, and we can get supplies to people faster." Paul and Joe looked over the plans and soon changed to faster river travel and trade. They were very busy getting new orders; thus, they had to purchase more steamboats and hire more men.

They soon found out steamboat travel was dangerous; explosions, sinking, Indian attacks, and daring steamboat races captured the country's imagination. Joe began to make more money and shared a profit with Paul.

At the end of each day, Paul and Dora ate at a restaurant before going home. They were both so exhausted that when they got home all they did was eat and go to sleep. Paul dropped Dora off at her home. She was too tired to kiss him at night. All she wanted was a bath and a bed.

Late on the afternoon of May 13th, as the Federals were poised to strike at Jackson, Mississippi, one of Paul's trains arrived in the capital city carrying Confederate General Joseph E. Johnston. President Jefferson Davis ordered him to the city to salvage the deteriorating situation in Mississippi. The train was loaded with ammunition for the men, but sheets of rain threatened to ruin the ammunition by soaking the powder in their cartridge boxes.

Meanwhile, Sherman's corps reached Lynch Creek southwest of Jackson at 11 a.m. and were immediately fired upon by Confederate artillery posts in the open fields north of the stream. Union cannons were hurried into position, and in short, orders drove the Confederates back into the city's defenses.

At 2:00 p.m., Paul was notified that the army's supply train had left Jackson and decided to withdraw his command until Paul ordered to get his train out of there.

Boys as young as nine were enlisting on both sides. Giving the Civil War the name "The Boy's War". Youths' enlistment into the armed forces was not a new phenomenon in the nineteenth century. President Abraham Lincoln sternly told them, "The United States doesn't need the service of boys who disobey their parents. The parents have to be with them to tell the child's age." Sadly, a lot of parents didn't know their age.

Five hundred of Joe Jenkins' men and many of the boys wanted to go to service. Some of the boys dishonestly signed their recruitment papers. The boys told the recruiters, "I am eighteen," when they were only fifteen, or sometimes even younger.

There were many ways that a young boy could get around the legal age limitations, the easiest route was to lie about their age to the recruitment officers. Pressured by their superiors, officers often turned a blind eye to the evident youth of willing recruits to fill their recruitment quotas. Other recruitment officers who were ministers would use their congregations as recruitment pools. Parishioners were less hesitant to let their boys enlist because good Christian gentleman led their regiment. Dora used her influence with local recruitment officers to enroll her students with the parent's permission.

At the time, boys were very good workers. If the boy couldn't get around a stubborn recruitment officer, the line of inquiry then turned to the boy's parents. If the boy was sixteen and ordered out of line, his father, who was right behind him, stepped in. The recruitment officers often heard, "he can work as steady as any man," and "he can shoot as straight as any man who signed up today," The officers didn't ask any more questions and just handed the boys a pen. The parents thought it would help the boy learn about the world and make him a man.

Joe had a lot of boys whose parents wouldn't give their consent. They would simply run away from home and enlist in another town. Some boys enlisted under a false name so their parents couldn't track them down and bring them back home to be a slave.

CHAPTER TWENTY-SEVEN

JOAN JOINS THE SERVICE

Joan is bored working in the fields and getting nowhere. She wants to see the world. She talks to Dora, "About joining the service. Dora doesn't want her to go because she will miss her."

Joan enlists Monday morning. She is aware that it is incredibly dangerous terrain. Black women often work as spies for the Yankees, carrying information from one major to another. This is very dangerous work. As a freedwoman who hated being a house slave, Joan Jenkins receives extracted information from one of the most important figures in the army - General Jefferson Davis.

Davis thinks that Joan is illiterate and possesses low cognitive abilities. She is far from that as she is very smart and has a photographic memory. She will retell all the information verbatim, along with any plans or memos she reads while cleaning the enemy house. Joan is a good seamstress and will be sewing messages in women's dresses belonging to the Davis household.

Joan comes back to Jim and Jane's home and tells them, "Bye, I am leaving tomorrow morning to be a spy and carry messages from general to general." Joan is small, and she can ride well and fast. She shows the general just how good she is.

The next morning Jim takes Joan to the station. As she steps down from the wagon, a piercing bugle blast precedes the sound of galloping horses going by her as she waves bye to Jim and walks over to Mazon Andy Johnson. He tears his eyes away from the Federal cavalry unit before him and takes Joan to his tent to give her a boy's uniform. He tells her about the danger she will be in and what she will be doing. Joan is ready to give her life to her hometown. She has been a slave all her life, and now she is prepared to see the wartime world.

Major Johnson does not worry about the welfare of his men, who were familiar enough with the land to evade the enemy no matter what the weather. He does worry about Joan in the line of fire.

Joan will be a spy watching in different places for the Union. Major Johnson sends a soldier with Joan for a couple of days to train her. Joan is so good at tracking the soldiers, and it is reported to Major Johnson just how good she is. Major Johnson gives Joan a pass and sends her out the next morning to track a troop about six miles from them. It is a rolling mass of dark-bellied clouds that launch her. She knows that the Union soldiers will stop and make tents in the storm. When she gets closer to the Union, she gets off her horse, Lighting. Then, she slowly crawls from tree to tree. She slowly puts her hand on her revolver at her hip when she hears a noise. One of the soldier boys is tying up his horse before walking away, back to his tent. She eases her hand away from her revolver but keeps her hand close. She listens to the talk of the men sitting around the fire and then slowly crawls back to her horse. She quietly and slowly walks out of the woods, trying not to make a sound.

Joan rides back to her unit to tell her Major everything she has heard. The men by the fire are talking about how, in the morning, at daylight, they will come up from the North and take the Federal Cavalry. She hears them saying that it is time for them to pay for the killing they had caused.

Joan is sent on another tracking trip to spy on troops. She possesses the skill of appearing, only to disappear into thin air. She knows how to guide men through the underbrush and around fallen trees, but, more importantly, how to lose them and leave them in a trap.

Joan needs a drink of water and comes upon a river of water. She asks Lighting, "How about a drink, old girl," as she slides down off of her saddle. She walks to the bank, bends down, and takes gulps of water by the handfuls.

She is unaware that someone is watching her at the stream. Her horse is eating grass by the bank.

The soldier rides quickly toward her with his gun out, ready to take her. Joan reaches for her revolver and blinks to make sure the fading daylight is not playing tricks on her vision. The soldier is big and older than she is. He cocks his weapon and shouts across the fast-moving stream, "Don't move!"

Joan stands and challenges him with a smile. "What do you want, sir?" The boy thinks to himself, can this be the Yankee's scout? I have chased a Yankee scout wearing an oversized coat, baggy trousers, and a slouch hat pulled low. This boy looks harmless enough. The soldier then looks at her horse, and this answers his question. He knows of very few horses in this part of the country, like this horse, certainly none of such quality that has not already been confiscated by one or the other armies. This is not a boy just on an evening ride. This is an enemy from the other side.

The boy tells her, "I think you know what I want. It appears we've spent the last week watching each other." The soldier keeps his gun on her as he rides his mare down the bank to a sandbar. She knows the creek is not wide, but it has swift-running current and slippery rocks. She tells him, "If I can offer you some advice, sir, this is not a safe place to cross." He doesn't listen to her and urges his horse forward into the ice-cold water. Then, he sees that he is in trouble. He gathers the reins, and the horse loses his footing and goes down. The boy tries to swim, but the current is too much for him, and he goes under. Joan jumps in and tries to save him. She can't save him, so she swims back to the bank and gets up onto her horse. She knows someone will come looking for him, and she doesn't want to be there when they do. She sees someone coming through the trees.

Lantern light reflects off the leaves, casting shadows on her. Joan slips back into the woods soaking wet and finds Lighting waiting on her. Slowly, she walks away through the woods, gets back up on her saddle, and rides off toward her group.

Someone screams, and Joan sees a rider. She decides that now is the time to ride and ride fast. She picks up the pace and rides, cutting back and forth through the trees to safety. The limbs are snagging her clothes, but she holds onto her reins tightly and endures the gasping and prickly of her skin. She knows that she has to move faster to evade capture.

Pain radiates through her as she steps down from her horse and twists her ankle on a fallen log. She lies flat on the ground for a few seconds in pain. She knows that she has to keep going. She crawls back to her horse and pulls herself up in the saddle. As she rides, she tells herself War is no game girl and starts riding faster. The storm has been bad, with the rain hitting her in the face. But now, the veil of clouds begins to part, throwing a sharp beam of light through the dense canopy. Joan holds her breath and peers around the tree, spotting her group of soldiers in front of her. As she rides as fast as she can, she is thanking God. The soldier at the gate hollers, "Open the gate," and lets her in.

As Joan travels through the gate, a piercing bugle blast precedes the sound off like galloping horses for mere seconds. Joan is riding Lighting; a large black horse and the horse jump at the sound. Joan rides her horse through the underbrush and around trees to Major Johnson's tent. It is raining, and she hears the distinctive sound of running water. Joan rides her horse up to the water and asks Lighting, "How about a drink, Ol'girl?" Lighting walks forward, leaning low to get a drink. Joan had been riding hard, as she looks up, she sees one of the soldiers. He reaches for his revolver and blinks to make sure the fading daylight is not playing tricks on his vision. Joan hollers at him, "Noel, it is me, Ace."

Noel looks at Joan dressed in an oversized coat, slouch hat pulled low and baggy trousers. He tells her, "You should have told me sooner, who you were." Noel knows as he looks at her horse as few such horses exist in this part of the country, certainly none of such quality.

Joan waves at him before walking up and going into Major Johnson's tent. Major Johnson continues writing even when Joan makes a noise. Joan hands him a crumpled message she retrieves out of an oak tree and lays it on his desk. He looks up at Joan and asks her, "What is this? Major Johnson picks up the note and reads it and looks up at Joan. "Is this true?" "Yes, Sir, I got it out of the oak tree from another spy." Joan stands in front of his desk waiting for his answer. He says after making her wait a few minutes, "What do you know of the other spy?" Joan takes a step closer and tells him," I know him from my childhood home at Jenkins Plantation. I will give my life for his word to be true. "I need to speak to you, Sir. I live at Jim and Jame Shell's home, near Vicksburg, Mississippi. He thinks to himself and realizes that he knows of the Shells, and they are very nice people.

"I understand, Sir, but I am sure it is true to its word." Joan is exhausted since she has been up for three days, and her vile breath tells him she is telling the truth.

Major Johnson sits on the corner of his desk as he crosses his arms. He looks at Ace and says, "You always tell the truth, even though this story is a bit incredible."

Joan tells him, "The risk is real, Sir."

Joan said, "I hear certain things all the time, and I have reason to believe you, have a spy within your ranks in your group." Major Johnson asks her," what possesses you to say such a thing?" "I can't tell you how I know, but my other spy tells me that the note was in the oak tree, Sir. As you can see, it has his numbers and name on the note." As Major Johnson strolls up to the fireplace and poles at the logs for a few moments, he thinks about what the note says. He again glances back at Joan standing by his desk and looks at her more closely. He can see that Joan has been riding all night, and her hair is tousled as if it had been days in the wind. She looks like she needs a good night's sleep. He is aware that Joan has the nickname "the Ace." He believes that Ace will go through extreme measures to give him the note. Major Johnson tells her, "It is harder for me to believe this information about this soldier?" "I understand, Sir, but I am sure it is true to its word." Again he could see Joan is exhausted since she has been up for three days, and her vile breath tells him she is telling the truth."

CHAPTER TWENTY-EIGHT

BAD MEN

The town has men watching the outskirt of town for outsiders. One of the boys watching runs inside the sheriff's office hollering on one a quite sunny day. "Sheriff Benny, Sheriff Benny, I was up on the hill, and I see five bad-looking men talking around a fire right outside of town. I slip up in the trees and hear them talking about robbing the bank here." The boy is looking toward the window of the jail, telling Sheriff Benny all about it. Sheriff Benny tells the boy to run and tell every man in town to come to the jail right now! Sheriff John has told Sheriff Benny about his bank being robbed just two days before.

Men start coming around in the front of the jailhouse with guns, and Sheriff Benny comes out the door with a shotgun in his hands and a pistol on each hip. He starts telling everyone to get themselves positioned in windows, on top of the building, and behind turned-over wagons and keep a watch for them. The town is surrounded by men on all sides. Ladies and children are told to go inside and not to come out for any reason.

The robbers are the James-Younger Gang just outside of the town on the Northside. Jesse James and his brother Frank James are outlaws. They usually commit these robberies many months apart, but it is only two days apart on this occasion. Jesse and Frank have Cole, Jim, John, and Bob joining them in on this robbery.

For nearly a decade, following the Civil War, the James-Younger Gang is among the most feared, most publicized, and most wanted confederations of outlaws on the American frontier. Sheriff Benny tells his men," The gang crimes are reckless and brutal; many gang members command notoriety in the public eye, which earns them significant popular support and sympathy. He tells the men, "We can't have any sympathy for these men. We must protect our women and children. They have robbed banks, trains, and stagecoaches in at least eleven states."

It is the first daylight when the outlaws ride into town. Everyone is ready for them. The James gang comes in shooting and tries to steal $60,000 in cash and bonds that have just come in on the train the day before. They kill an outsider on the street by the bank. The men in town start shooting and shooting two of the men. Dora is in the train office next to the bank and is under her desk. She is afraid they are going to come inside the office. Paul runs into the office looking for her and tells her to stay under the desk as he retrieves his rifle.

The James and Younger brothers belong to slave-owning families from an area known as "Little Dixie" in western Missouri with strong ties to the South. Dora learns that Frank and Jesse James's mother, Zereida Samuel, is an outspoken partisan of the South, though the Youngers' father, Henry Washington Younger, is believed to be a Unionist. Cole Younger's initial decision to fight as a bushwhacker is attributed to his father's death at the hands of Union forces in July 1862.

Dora read that Jessie and Frank James had found under one of the most famous Confederate bushwhackers. Jesse James begins his guerrilla career in 1864, at the age of sixteen, fighting alongside Frank under the leadership of Archie Clement and "Bloody Bill" Anderson.

Sheriff Benny and his men chase the James gang out of their town but are afraid they may be back. The bank is safe, for now. The men successfully kill one and wounding two of the gang members. Sheriff Benny tells the men, "We have to stand watch. We have two of their men, and I am sure they will be back."

Paul helps Dora out from under the desk. She is so scared she runs into his arms crying. Paul puts his arms around her and tells her that everything is ok now. The gang is gone. They didn't get the train shipment of money brought in yesterday on one of his trains. What he didn't tell her is that they may be back.

Sheriff Benny orders men to take watch around the town on twelve hours shifts and report to him anything they see out of order.

Two months later, Jessie and Frank rob one of Paul's trains at Gads Hill, Missouri, and Pinkerton's National Detective Agency is contacted to hunt them down. Allan Pinkerton, a Scottish immigrant, serves as the first full-time detective on Windy City's police force. The private agency has experience in capturing train robbers after the agency takes on the case of the James gang. A Pinkerton, a detective, is searching for Jesse and Frank in Missouri and wound up dead. Another Pinkerton agent who pursues the brothers' fellow gang members Cole and Robert Younger in another part of the state is also shot.

Catching the James brothers becomes a personal mission for Allan Pinkerton. He is an abolitionist who aided slaves on the Underground Railroad. He uncovers a plot to assassinate President-elect Abraham Lincoln and gathers military intelligence for the federal government during the Civil War.

Shortly after midnight in January, a group of Pinkerton agents, acting on a tip that Jesse and Frank are at their mother's farm, carry out a raid on the place. The agents throw an incendiary device into the farmhouse. This sets off an explosion that fatally wounds Jesse and Frank's 8- year-old half-brother and causes their mother to lose part of her arm. Jessie and Frank are not found there.

Sheriff Benny is told that the James gang is coming back to Sheriff John's town. They are bringing Cole, Jim, and Robert with them. They try to rob the First National Bank. After learning that a former Union general and the Republican governor of Reconstruction-era Mississippi has recently moved to Vicksburg, Mississippi, the gang targets the bank. The train has brought in $75,000 and deposited it in the bank. During the attempted robbery, three gang members are inside and demand the cashier opens the safe. He refuses. Meanwhile, after townspeople outside get wind that a holdup is taking place, they engage in a shootout with the gang members. In the end, the bank cashier is killed by the outlaws, as was a passerby, while two bandits are shot to death by townsfolk before the rest of the gang flees.

Two weeks later, following a gunfight near Arkansas, the Younger brothers are captured, and another gang member is killed. Sheriff John tells Sheriff Benny "that the Youngers are sentenced to life in prison." Everyone in both towns is glad the robbers are put in prison for life. Sheriff John writes Sheriff Benny a couple of years later and tells him 'that Robert Younger died behind bars in 1889. This sibling was paroled in 1901.

CHAPTER TWENTY-NINE

TRAINS COLLIDE HEAD-ON

On the morning of October 19, 1862, the paperboy runs into Paul's office with the newspaper. Paul is fixing his coffee. He hasn't heard the news yet. Paul walks over to his desk as he is drinking his coffee. He sits down and picks up the morning paper. On the front page is the story about one of his trains having a head-on collision in Duck Hill, Mississippi. As he reads, he couldn't believe the news. He stands up and shakes his head. In the morning hours, two trains collided head-on, killing thirty-four men. Most of the dead are Confederate soldiers. It is the South's worst loss of life in a train accident.

Duck Hill is a thriving mill town after geologists locate iron ore nearby. Paul is making millions on iron ore. Paul has had a railroad robbery on his trains. Two armed men, Rube Burrow and Joe Jackson clung to the outside of one of his trains as it leaves the station; they then climb into the engine cabin. They order the engineer to stop the train about a mile north of town. The robbers plunder the express car's safe of $3000 and kill one man who tries to intervene.

Paul tells Dora to hire three detectives and a sheriff named Sheriff Pennington of Lamar County, and the party proceeds to Veron, the county seat. On the early morning of January 10th, they decide to raid the home of Jim Burrow. Jim Burrow resides in a small dwelling with his family about four miles from Vernon. The men hope to find both Rube and Jim. The detectives are on horseback, and Sheriff Jerry is the guide. Sheriff Pennington and the detectives are in a wagon with McGinn. The party

213

drives to a point the guide designates as a half-mile from Jim Burrow's house. They leave a guard in charge of the horses, and the posse quietly surrounds the house. They are closing in upon the place just as dawn is approaching. The guide informs the detectives that he has the posse at the wrong house. He points to another house about a half-mile away. As the men arrive at the second house, the guide realizes that he made another error. It was then daylight. The detectives are about to withdraw and get their horses and wagon out of the way before they are discovered when they find the inmates of the house already observed them. They then proceed about three miles further on, and then they come given Jim Burrow's residence.

As the men come within about a hundred and fifty yards of Jim's house, the outlaw discovers them and realizes at once that a posse is in pursuit of him. Jim dashes through the rear door of the house and runs for the timber. He reaches the woods unscathed. He is followed by a fusillade from the ranks of the officers.

Jim gets away, and he boards a train. As the train is pulling into a depot, an officer is waiting for him. It is raining hard. The officer is wearing a long, loose rubber coat and a broad-brim slouch hat. The hat is well-drawn down over his face as he tries to conceal his features. The conductor tells the officer, "I think that is Jim and his brother walking down the track toward our train."

When the officers inform the boys they are under arrest, Jim Burrow stumbles and falls after making a break for liberty, and in the next instant, two officers are upon him. Paul receives the money that Burrow stole from his train, but he has lost good men in the robbery.

When Dora comes into the office, Paul tells her all about the train wreck and the stolen money. As Paul and Dora walk out the door that evening, Paul tells her, " I hope this is the last we hear about a train robbery."

CHAPTER THIRTY

THE SOLDIERS ARE COMING

John Ben and Little Frank are playing cowboys and Indians with their cap guns by the river. It is John Ben's 8th birthday, but he doesn't have a birthday cake or a party because things are tough with the raging war. So, he celebrates his birthday with his cousin Little Frank. John Ben tells his mother, "I hope by my next birthday we will have peace in our land so that I can have a nice dinner and party."

John Ben is hiding behind a tree shooting at Little Frank when he looks down the river. He hears loud noises coming toward him. John Ben and Little Frank run to the back door of the Jenkins Plantation and holler to the cook, "The Yankees are coming to our house, and they will capture Little Frank and me." John Ben and Little Frank run and hide under the bed with their guns. Union soldiers invade Pam's home and demand food. Sally gives them food to eat. One of the men approaches the bed where the boys were. Finding it warm, he accuses Pam of harboring and concealing a wounded rebel in a dreadful language. He swears that he will leave the rebel soldier's heart's blood." He stoops to look under the bed and sees the little white figures crouching in a distant corner. He grabs them by one foot and drags them forth.

Little Frank is too terror-stricken to cry but clasps his little cap gun fast to his throbbing little heart. The soldier wrenches both forms from under the bed and thrusts the little boys away with such violence that Pam falls against the bed. After feeding the soldiers, Sally and Sue run to find Pam in the knitting room. She is already watching out the window holding the two boys to her chest.

Many of the characteristics of Pam's ideas have been and continue to be essential to the myth of the Southern lady. Pam is familiar with the Antebellum American culture; the Southern lady maintains an elusive; yet, powerful presence. She has become the ideal female figure belonging to a specific race and class in the white middle class of Southerners.

It is among her race and class that the myth of the Southern lady first originates. This serves as a manifestation of the cultural attitudes of the South as well as a guide to how upper-class women are to behave and present themselves in the domestic and social sphere.

Before the war, everyone gives the plantation mistress the attention and recognition she deserves. Pam is responsible for most domestic tasks and the care and feeding of both the white and Black inhabitants of the plantation. Pam is both refined and virtuous to reflect the public perception of their class and social position. But now that the war is raging, she has to work in the fields and help clean the plantation.

Even though Pam helps with everything, there is a clear class priority and racial struggles over gender struggles. Slave women do not necessarily share their mistresses' opinions about slavery and view them as oppressors. Even though the white women and Black slave women of the South work together, there is still a distinctive gap in their experiences.

Pam finds the task of directly supervising and disciplining slaves to be a difficult thing. At times, the slaves show her respect and do exactly as she requests of them. In other instances, they disobey her. Pam, nevertheless, makes the hard decisions regarding her slaves. She serves as more than just a placeholder for her husband while he was off fighting in the war.

Pam has her ideas of what a woman can be as a wife, mother, and businesswoman. Pam works hard to ensure the success of Jenkins Plantation while her husband is fighting.

The Civil War period is a time of immense changes and adjustments for Pam. The Civil War disrupts and alters her life. In some cases, her prewar life is lost forever. As Pam sits in her living room, she thinks how, before the war, her life was about conforming to the strict Southern code of womanhood. This ideal of womanhood is essential for young, proper elite women cultivating purity, domesticity, and submissiveness. These traditional standards include accepting her role in the patriarchal system. White elite men have power over women, lower-class whites, and slaves. But as she looks down at her raw hands, now the demands of war offer elite Confederate women the opportunity to be a part of the struggle for Southern independence. And like their men, these women define themselves as "independent" Southern women. As Pam looks down at her raw hands, she wants to cry, but she knows that she has to be strong for Joe.

She knows women have to be supportive and confident in both the new Confederacy and the men who fight for it. Pam knows she has to carry on the plantation and survive the war. She has to fulfill a "mother" role on the plantation to John Ben. The self-sacrifice for her is to be the maternal figure for both her child and her slave dependents. Pam depends on the slave system when the demands of the plantation wife also increase. She has to provide for her husband's slaves with food, clothing, shelter, and medical care. She knows she has to prioritize the importance of caring for her slaves."

Joe has been the ruler of all that happens on his property, but he isn't here now. Pam is the head of the household now and is expected to maintain social order on the plantation and exert dominance over the slaves. Yet, as the war progresses, Pam experiences challenge in her way of life. With Joe in the Confederate army, Pam finds herself trying to control slaves for the first time. Pam feels helpless because she does not command the same authority as Joe does. Sometimes she questions whether slavery is worth the trouble it causes. She wants Joe to come home.

As more and more men leave for the battlefield, women find themselves doing all the work in a world of white women and Black slaves. Pam feels the responsibility of managing slaves is an unwaning burden. This causes her to question the moral and political legitimacy of the institution.

By 1864, Pam's husband joins for a week's furlough. Joe is fighting for the Union. She hopes he will not return to the front and writes to a friend: "Do not call me unpatriotic, May! I am sure farmers are as necessary to our suffering country as soldiers. Food and clothing must be available for the army as well as for the women and children. Starvation is a more powerful foe than those we are now contending with."

Pam has to release a lot of her slaves. The Union spirits away African American labor; men as soldiers and women as cooks and laundresses. African Americans also serve as nurses in government hospitals, supplied wagons, and ambulances, and cooked and valet within Confederate camps. The masters donate and supervise their slaves. Most importantly, the War Department often does not have the authority to impress slave labor into service.

Pam doesn't have many of her family slaves because they engage in wartime service. Pam's mom and dad now live with her and her children because their home burnt down. Slaves remain at the root of the problem during the prolonged battle for Southern independence. Only in the last few weeks of the war has the Confederate government willing to consider arming Blacks in a desperate bid to continue the losing battle.

John Ben and Little Frank are crying. The war is teaching the children some terrible lessons.

The slaves are in the fields picking cotton and stop to watch as the soldiers march through. Mississippi plays a pivotal role in the war. The population of Mississippi is seven hundred and ninety-one thousand people. The slaves in Mississippi outnumber the whites by four hundred and thirty-seven thousand to three hundred and fifty-four thousand. Slavery, therefore, is an absolute necessity for the state's white citizens. White soldiers are marching through the mud four-mile wide and two miles long!

White soldiers from Mississippi reflect the state's position on slavery. Yet, they often fight for a variety of other reasons. Some join the military to defend homes and hearth, while others see the conflict in broader sectional terms. The soldiers' motivation is generally more personal than it is ideological.

Pam knows white and Black soldiers from Mississippi contribute to both the Union and Confederate war efforts, fighting within the state and as far away as the battle of Gettysburg in Pennsylvania. She and Joe just read this morning that around eighty thousand white men from Mississippi fight in the Confederate Army. In contrast, five hundred white Mississippians fought for the Union. More than seventeen thousand Black Mississippi slaves and freedmen fight for the Union. At this time, you will read more about the white soldier than the Black soldiers.

Joe has lost more than sixty slaves enlisting to fight. He and Pam are using children as young as six to work the crops. By as early as 1863, the floodgates of freedom are open wide to African Americans who seize the opportunity to escape their masters. This disintegrating process undermines the resolve of Confederates, especially non-slave owners who form the majority of the fighting force. For those left behind on plantations, the process is even more painful to witness, as the spirit of emancipation creates not so much a tidal wave of resistance as a strong and constant flow that washes over the South. This continuous flow erodes slaveholders' power with the sands of time, day by day. Without slaves, many southern fields and plantations are intended.

Sally and Sue's husbands are fighting for the North. Sally receives a letter from John. He says, " Hi darling, it is a very bad morning, and raining hard again. I am fighting every day, and one of my friends is killed. It has been raining for two days. It will turn cold after a while. I am out all night fighting and in my fox hole trying to get some sleep. Love you, John."

Joan writes to Jim and Jane comments, "that she is ok" as she watches the Union soldiers report back to their Captain. Civil War soldiers are among the most literate in history. About eight out of every ten Confederate soldiers and nine out of every ten Union soldiers can read and write. The letters and diaries that Union and Confederate soldiers have written bequeath to scholars in the field the unusual problem of having an overabundance of firsthand accounts to consult.

Joan writes about the groundbreaking work on soldiers. How the conflict unfolds and what it meant to participants. Joan will write letters on her knees and thighs, for that is all she has in the woods. She will write on anything that she has access to, on the backs of military forms, old brown paper, and letters from home. Joan can read and write, and she will not write letters for others when she can teach them to read and write.

Soldiers are more likely to write letters during their first months of service, and they have more time and amenities for writing while in camp.

John, Sally's husband, musters in the Confederate service; from 1861 to 1865, he serves as a private and sergeant in the Maury Artillery Battery.

During the war, John writes a memorandum; the content elaborates burdens of contact with the Yankees. Pam tells her husband, "They tear my earrings you bought me out of my ears. One soldier took my wedding rings, and when I fought him, he threw me down the stairs and knocked me about. One of them tells me they shot ladies as well as men. If I do not stop talking and displaying my confederate flag, he will blow my brains out."

Before they leave Pam's home, fifteen thousand bales of government cotton go up in flames. Pam tells Joe, "They take our heads of cattle and a thousand head of hogs with them. The Yankees strip us bare of everything to eat! They drive off all the cattle, mules, and horses; they kill chickens and turn their horses into our wheat field. They feed their houses and tramp the rest down." As Pam cries in Joe's arms, she tells him, "They come into the house and search it several times and steal several of my things." She tells him, "How they drag John Ben and Little Frank out from under the bed and scare them."

"We have to wash the walls. They threaten the women slaves with the worst treatment. They write all over the walls addressing the women slaves as if they were writing a letter. They write many pieces of obscenity."

One of the slave ladies tells Joe, "I am nursin' my baby when I hear a gallopin', and before I could move, here come the Yankees riding up...The officer might have been a general. He snaps off his hat and bows low to me and asks my baby's name."

As the soldiers march down the Mississippi, the Black youth on the plantation find the whole idea of war exotic and intriguing. Sue goes with the white children and watches the soldiers marching. The drums are playing, and the next thing she hears, the soldiers at war are marching on. You can listen to the guns just as plain as day. The soldiers go by in droves from sunup till sundown. Sue's children are under ten and are out working in the fields that day. They watch as the soldiers go by.

Many Black children sacrifice their parents to the terrible conflict. As slave men and boys flee the plantations, they leave their wives and children behind. Thousands are these families fatherless, and hundreds are orphaned.

Pam knows some women will die before they complain to any man in the army. She tries not to complain. She knows Joe has enough to bear without that. But after years of seeing Joe leave, no amount of sanity can prevent him from understanding the dire straits on the home front.

Women and children ARE starving. They will get together with other ladies and go to the bakeries, and each of them will take a loaf of bread. The government has little to give us because they horde it for the fighting men. Nearly a thousand women and children in our town band together and march along silently and orderly. They methodically empty stores of goods and refuse to stop even when the mayor confronts them to read the "Riot Act." Forty-eight hours later, an observer reports, "Women and children are still standing in the streets with Pam, demanding food, and the government is issuing rations of rice to us."

Women and children are praying in churches. Christian faith gives these women their redemption as well. All the women are struggling to find some sense of the slaughter of their husbands. God have mercy on our land and graves.

Pam can't believe it. Her nerves are frayed, her supplies disappeared, and the Yanks maintain their attacks. Scurvy, mule-skinning, and bombardment chip away at her morals. Her wounded animals limp around looking for grass. As she tries to sleep, the nightly shelling keeps her frightened child awake. She takes John Ben to her bed and holds him all night.

Her challenges are tremendous, and daily life is hard for her, on occasion, deadly. She has to do a lot of work in the fields and barn. Her hands are raw using hoe-cropping cotton.

After the soldiers leave Pam's home, the women stand and look at each other as though staring across a battlefield. Their faces register a range of emotions such as sadness, anger, and even resignation. All their work is up in smoke. As one woman looks to the left, Pam stands in profile, a study in sharp angular planes despite her feminine ruffled collar. To her right, a group of African American women returns her stare. Their bodies turn outward so that they appear to root in one place.

Pam will work right along with the slave women cleaning, laundering, and cooking. A lot of enslaved women often seek work outside the home before the end of Reconstruction. They are also working in the field as labor in the form of sharecropping.

Pam works along with the other ladies from sunup to sundown... They all bear heavy loads of cotton and are all shabbily dressed. One young woman gazes somberly into the distance. The women of color are poor and continued in poverty after the Civil War and the failure of the Reconstruction to change living conditions for slave women fundamentally.

The government is going to give the slaves something, but they never do. In addition to their hard struggles, free women face little change in social conditions and confront increased racial hostility.

Pam's mom June and her dad Ben are living with her. On returning to her home from the barn, an explosion sounds near her. She hears one wild scream, and she runs into the house. Her mother is sinking like a wounded dove, the lifeblood flowing over the light summer dress in crimson ripples from a deadly wound on her side the result of a shell fragment. A fragment also strikes and breaks the arm of her dad standing near her mother. She is heart-wrenching, crying for her parents as she sits on the floor holding her mother to her chest.

Pam has to watch them bury her mother by the fence. It is hard for her. As the preacher says a prayer over her mother, Pam can't stand up and sits down on the ground, overcome with grief. Joe comes home for the funeral, picks Pam up, carries her to the house, and lays her on their bed. Pam cries for days and doesn't want to get up or eat. Joe worries about her and calls the doctor. Joe has to go back to war the next morning. Doctor Baker tells him he sees a lot of this. He tells Joe, "She will be alright in time. You must go back."

Pam is visiting her husband in Vicksburg when she is trapped by the advancing Yankee army closing in on Vicksburg from the east. She becomes a cave dweller during the siege and leaves the following account.

"Pam gets out of her wagon and hides the wagon and horse. She fits the cave with articles of housekeeping just in case she couldn't get home. She arranges to bed her upon planks, and she improvises to elevate the stand. Planks cover the ground floor, and these, in turn, she covers with matting and carpets for her and her son. She also covers the surrounding wall with strips of carpets. This is to eliminate as much dampness as possible. She secures the wall carpeting with small wooden pins."

Pam and her son John Ben claw into the cave and put the branches in front to hide the hole. She doesn't have a light as she is too afraid the soldiers will see it when they ride by. They never see her, and the next morning Pam and her son climb out of the cave, get their wagon out of the limbs, and ride home.

After millions of people lose their lives and homes, Lee's surrender on April 9, 1865, ends the Confederate dream. The preservation of the Union gives Lincoln hope, a hope cut short by his assassination on April 14. Following Lincoln's wishes, the country rapidly tries to reunite and heal the bitter wounds of four years of fratricide. Struggling back to peacetime is an enormous effort in the North but an even more devastating prospect for white Southerners.

Over ten billion dollars worth of property is destroyed in the region, like Joe and Pam's home. African Americans rejoice in Confederate defeat. The passage of the Thirteen Amendment in December 1865 abolishes slavery.

After the war, transportation, and industrialization once again boomed for Joe and Paul. In the North, only the textile industry suffers. Paul sends coal production, copper processing, and other resources on his trains. For Joe, the back of the plantation economy has been broken, and there seems to be no way to restore prewar patterns, despite planters' dreams. The Black workforce is reluctant to return to former plantations. Most want to escape fieldwork and the whipping. In the past, Joe is good at his work and never whips them. Since they lack education and resources, they come back and work for the daily wage labor pay. Each plantation owner has to give each man slave "forty acres and a mule." This is a dream for each slave as he can work for his master and then work on his land.

Reconstruction gives African Americans their first taste of freedom, and many seize the moment with vigor and admirable restraint. The way Southern Blacks struggle for their rights and stepped lively into political arenas is one of the great political transformations of the millennium. Former slaves shed their shackles and bid for their full and rightful place in public life.

Nevertheless, the costs of the war are enormous. Joan is coming home to Jim and Jane, and they can't wait to see her. She is a spy and sees almost six hundred and thirty thousand deaths, with over half a million wounded. When she returns to Vicksburg, Mississippi, she is happy to see Jim, Jane, and Dora waiting for her at the station.

Once the war was over in April 1865, many families face the harsh reality that their husbands and brothers, fathers and sons may not come home. A lot of the men are without legs and arms. Tens of thousands have not heard from families for months or even years and find their inquiries to the government War Department fall on deaf ears. The government is flooded with requests following the Confederate surrender. Thousands of men are buried in anonymous graves.

The end of the war in 1865 brings a welcoming peace, especially for the men serving as soldiers. Armies disband, and regiments muster out of service. Former soldiers return to the farms and stores they left so long ago. But the memories of their service and old comrades do not disappear quite so rapidly. In the decade following the end of the Civil War, organizations of veterans of the North and South are formed. Northern veterans join the Grand Army of the Republic, and Confederate veterans enroll in the United Confederate Veterans.

Joe comes home without one of his limbs. He is shot in the right arm. Doctors amputate his shattered limb close to the shoulder. The Civil War kills and injures over a million Americans, roughly a third of all those who serve. This count, however, doesn't include the conflict's psychological wounds on men.

The doctors have little grasp of how war can scar minds as well as bodies. Mental illnesses are also a source of shame, especially for soldiers bred on Victorian notions of manliness and courage. Wounded men who survive combat are subject to premodern medicine, including tens of thousands of amputations like Joe, with unsterile instruments. During the long stretches in crowded and unsanitary camps, men are haunted by the prospect of an agonizing and inglorious death away from the battlefield; diarrhea is among the most common killers.

Joe is on the 16th. The Confederates capture him and send him to the notorious Confederate prison at Andersonville. This is where a third of the men die from disease, exposure, and starvation. Jim arrives home weak, thin, and without one of his arms.

Pam is just so glad Joe is home. It is impossible to measure the human costs of the Civil War, the hardships, and the suffering. Pam is aware of all she has lost but having Joe home is a blessing. Joe observes women grieving for losing their loved ones when they discover they aren't coming home.

Joe tells Pam, "A little town in Brewster Country was shot up. There were some American soldiers stationed there, and they fought back. Now there are holes in the walls of those adobe buildings."

One of Joe's friends expects to die from the wounds he receives at the Second Battle of Petersburg in the summer of 1864. He sits with Joe in the parlor, and they talk about how he doesn't die. A bullet enters his right hip, tears through his lower abdomen, and exits his left hip. The field surgeons are afraid he isn't going to make it.

Joe is lucky because he has slaves to work his farms while he works in the office. Wheat farmers make a lot of money during this war. The price of wheat increases greatly during this time, and Joe is there to make money on both sides. Joe's steamboats during the Civil War win little glamour but play a critical role. Rivers serve as the lifeblood of the Confederacy; steamboats permit the rapid movement of heavy cargo up and down the waterways. Both Union and Confederate forces in Arkansas rely on steamboats to move troops and supplies. In essence, steamboats make the war effort possible.

Joe has flatboats and keelboats to move agricultural products downriver to New Orleans, Louisiana, but neither type of boat could easily make the return journey upstream coming back up. Paul's flatboats were typically broken up for lumber in New Orleans, while diminutive keelboats bring only a few goods back to Arkansas at a very slow pace.

Steamboats are less expensive to operate than Paul's trains. Paul works on an existing pathway of the navigable river system because of the fuel he harvests from Arkansas's abundant forests.

Joan saves hundreds of soldiers' lives as she helps them back to camp. Joan fights military red tape throughout the war. She sidesteps the chain of command and launches a personal crusade- she is fighting for what is right! Joan's military name is Ace, and she wants to do her part. She can ride Lighting and locate information on dying men, soliciting soldiers who may witness a comrade's passing so she can convey the details of the dead to her commander. She will dress like a girl and venture into enemy lines. She will sift through enemy records, listen in on them talking, and take the information back to her commander. The information consists of the location of thousands of buried soldiers, especially those who perish in prisons. This important information informs the wives that their husbands are not coming home and informs the government that a veteran has passed away.

Joan sits in the living room with Jim, Jane, and Dora and tells them, "This war takes an enormous emotional toll on all of us. Children lose their childhoods working in the fields, families lose loved ones, and the nation mourns the passing of a generation of youth who could have talents and energies and not just their bodies to their beloved country". Joan has tears in her eyes as she speaks of all the boys she buries on the battlefield. She elaborates on how she has to listen to the dying boys as they take their last breaths. "I still live with the memories, the words of soldiers, and love ones continue to haunt me." Jane and Dora hug Joan with tears in their eyes for all she had gone through.

CHAPTER THIRTY-ONE

JOAN COMES HOME

Jim begins turning his horse and wagon off the path to the mansion. As Jim rides the horse up to the house, Joan notices this place is a thing of singular beauty and looks different from when she left.

The yard smells of red and yellow roses, and there is a carpet of velvet grass. She hasn't walked on grass like this since she left three years ago. The sun fairly gleans from the boards of the front of the house, with roses covering the front of the house, making it lovely just to stop and look at it. The magic of the breeze makes Joan feel she is part of a dream and doesn't want to wake up. As Joan steps down from the wagon, she reaches down to pick up her bag as she looks at the scene. This is her home. Her dream cannot equate to the perfection of beauty that stands before her.

Joan can't believe with all that she had been through, there is still a place as beautiful as this. Joan allows her breath to escape her in a loud sigh of exasperation as she thinks of the many battles she was in as a spy and how she had to fight to achieve her renowned reputation as a fighter. She walks over to the bench by the river as she remembers the last days of fighting.

To her troops, she is a spy until the last day of the war. She takes them through a passage through the river, which is the only way out. She has to kill men on the Northside before one of them kills her Lieutenant.

As they escape and make it to a house in the South, a dispatcher brings a letter from Lee stating that the war is over. The North is celebrating with gunfire, and bells are ringing all over the U.S.A. It is a great night for the North but a sad one for the South. So many men have died!

Jane walks up behind Joan and sits next to her. Joan's face becomes obvious; her face is kindling with the same type of fire that burns when she is on the battlefield. Jane takes her hand in hers and tells her, "It is over, Joan. it will take time, but it is over."

Joan looks into Jane's face and informs her, "It is not over, Jane. I have to report to General Lee and President Davis in the morning. I am a spy for Major Johnson taking messages back and forth. Even though the war is over, we still have men out there who aren't happy about it. I leave notes for Major Johnson in trees. He doesn't know that I am a woman, but he will in the morning. He thinks a woman's place is in the home and not on the battlefield."

Monday morning at 8:00, she heads to the office of President Davis. General Lee is sitting by his desk. "Joan Shell reporting, sir!"

"At ease," Davis tells her." Private Shell this morning Major Johnson joins us. As you are aware, he does not know you are a woman leaving him messages. We think it is time to tell him."

"Yes, Sir," Joan says.

Major Johnson paces the foyer of Confederate President Jefferson Davis's home. He silently rehearses his proposal. He has no idea why they summon him to Richmond; but, he intends to use the opportunity to talk to Davis about the ending of the war and what's next.

Johnson tries to calm his jittery nerves. He doesn't know what is in store for him now that the war is over. He wants to know the identities of the spies and scouts that operate in his territory. The fact is that he does not have access to this information, and he does not understand why. As Major Johnson is walking back and forth, he pauses for a moment. Johnson strained his ears at the sound of voices floating down the staircase from the second-floor office. The president's butler informs him that Davis is having a meeting with General Lee. Yet, he can hear a woman's voice.

Johnson can't believe that a WOMAN has an interview with the president. At this time, it is impossible and ridiculous. Johnson stands up when he hears voices moving closer. He hears the distinct sound of a woman's voice. He stands erect with anticipation, waiting now for the source. Then, a woman's attire becomes visible to him. As she is coming down the stairs in a uniform, she tells President Davis, "Yes, Sir."

As General Lee steps off the bottom step, he sees Major Johnson. "Major Johnson! "

President Davis enters the room and tells Major Johnson, "I like you to meet Ace! Major Johnson looks at Joan. President Davis tells him, "Do you know, sir, who this woman is?"

Major Johnson tells him, "No Sir," as he looks at Joan.

"Allow me to introduce you formally. Major Johnson. I have the honor to introduce you to Joan Shell, better known as Ace, your scout."

Major Johnson's face reddens, "I know you were in my office as a boy as an annoyance. You blind my eyes to all things save his anger. A woman! I have been getting messages from a woman! This is an outrage! Why wasn't I told!" He cannot believe that he is a woman's target. This woman had been leaving him messages in a hollow oak tree for the past four months.

General Lee knows Joan as Ace. Joan is staring into space as Major Johnson babbles on and on. Joan is aware that her true identity is a secret to Major Johnson. It does not alarm her about the unexpected encounter with the man standing before her. President Davis tells Major Johnson, "No one is to know of her as a woman except the four of us." Major Johnson still can't believe it.

"Do you expect me to entrust myself and my men to her? A slave woman that only knows how to clean dishes?"

President Davis looks into Major Johnson's eyes. He points his finger at him and tells him, "She has done a great job saving your life for the past four months!"

Major Johnson tells him, "Yes, Sir!"

"Then, I do not want to hear any more about this. Do you understand, Major? "

"Yes, Sir."

Joan stands completely composed and doesn't say a word as Major Johnson marches out of the room. Joan has been a scout for three years and is aware of military tactics and how to keep secrets very well. General Lee assures Johnson that Ace has done a great detriment to her name.

As Major Johnson walks back to his horse Silver, he thinks this is not a woman's work. Surely, they can't expect me to accept communications from this woman. She needs to be at home taking care of the children. President Davis tells him, "To treat Ace with the respect and honor she deserves as an officer in your command. She is your scout until I tell you differently, is that clear!"

Joan Shell, Ace is to be Major Johnson's scout and protect his life with her own whether he likes it or not. Major Johnson tells her, "You better do a great job for me."

Joan informs him, "I will render my life for you, Sir. I have been a scout for three years and have not lost getting a message to a major yet!"

Johnson looks at her and tells her, "And you better not be with me. Despite my better judgment, it appears I will have to accept the circumstances thrust upon me by the president."

Joan smugly tells him, "Thank you, Major." Joan is trying to keep her composure in front of a man she knows would never think of her as anything more than a woman in a uniform with a gun.

Joan looks back at the gentlemen and tells them, "I have work to do. Will that be all?" Joan walks out and gets back up on Lighting, and heads for the forest, her home. She learned how to live in the forest over the past three years. A few minutes later, Ace looks up in the sky and notices dark clouds to the North of her. She knows that she is fixing to get wet as she reaches for her raincoat to put around her shoulders.

Joan knows better than anyone that traveling through Mississippi at this time alone is more dangerous than before. She lives in this enemy land all her life as a slave and as a scout. She has to do whatever she has to do to protect herself, her Major, and his men, even if it means giving her life for them.

President Davis tells Joan that Lincoln has plans for movement in the region they are in. Joan is aware that Major Johnson is not like most officers as he is strict and whatever he says is the gospel. His men worship him, and whatever he says. Joan is very stubborn and is just like him. When she is giving an order, sometimes she will change the order her way.

Joan is wet to the bone and her clothes are soaking wet! She finds a grove of trees to hide under. She desperately needs a nap. She has been riding for two days, and she is exhausted from a lack of sleep. Just as she closes her eyes, Lighting makes a noise to let her know someone is close by. She crawls between the trees as three soldiers ride up and stop to talk. One soldier is telling the other two, "We need to make camp down the road. The Yankees are within a mile of us. We need to take every one of them at dawn." Joan waits until they move on down the road. She claws to Lighting and takes his reins and leads him through the trees. She has to get to Major Johnson before it was too late.

It is midnight. Major Johnson removes his boots and sits down behind his desk to go over some papers. He plans to move out in the morning. As he loosens the collar of his shirt, he still cannot believe that a woman is his scout. He shakes his head in disgust! What will his men think when they hear of this?

He pours himself some coffee when he hears his aide's voice. "Excuse me, Sir?"

Johnson doesn't look up as he asks him, "What is it, Jacob? I am trying to go over these papers before sunup."

"Sir, there's someone here to see you, and they say it is important." Major Johnson looks up and instructs his aid to send him in. Major looks back down at his map on his desk, deciding where to go next.

"Major Johnson, I have a very important message for you," Joan says as she walks toward his desk. "I have been riding hard to get here. There is no other way to deliver this by morning." Joan has mud all over her, and she is wearing a boy's uniform with old boots caked with mud. Major Johnson looks her up and down. "I am sorry about the mud, sir, but I had to claw through the woods."

Major Johnson notices this woman had guts as he questions, "You have no horse?" She tells him, "I have to travel most of the way by foot, so the enemy doesn't see me. I am here because I hear some men talking about torching your friend's homes at daylight this morning. Her voice was neither excited nor frightening as she walks over to his desk where the map is. "I heard them speak these words three hours ago. Please, excuse me for being so muddy, but I have to crawl most of the way," as she points to a map on his desk.

"Most of the Yankee's troops will be leaving this area." She immediately points to the area she is talking about. "Captain Stewards moves here to torch homes and barns. The people only have ten minutes to get out beforehand. I hear them mention that Major David is here, to the North, to do the same thing while others will be going toward the South to do the same. They know that these families are assisting you in any way they can."

Major Johnson walks over to his desk to look at the map where she is pointing. Johnson says, "Do you see the men here? This is useless because there are direct roads between us."

Joan tells him, "I can get you through, surprise them with the attack, and get out before they know what happens to them."

Major Johnson looks at her. He hesitates a minute as he looks at her again, "I know you are not going to like me saying this, but I feel that a battlefield isn't any place for a woman."

Without any sarcasm in her voice, she tells him, "Sir, I am just as good of a fighter as any of your men. I can do my job better by myself without any help from your men."

He tells her, "This is no game, Miss Shell. I am not about to send you out in the enemy path alone. As headstrong as you are, I am going to have two of my men accompany you. Do you understand, Miss Shell? If the enemy catches you, they will hang you as a spy."

Joan looks deeply into his eyes and tells him, "That is of little concern to me. Are you going to try to stop me from going by myself, Sir?"

Major Johnson looks at her and threatens, " I will tie you up if I have to."

Joan informs him, "that the main roads are picketed and the minor ones patrolled. How will you get through? As he steps in front of her. Joan tells him, "I have lived here all my life, and I am very familiar with the land. I use to go through this area to see my boyfriend at night, and no one ever caught me."

Major Johnson laughs and cocks his head to look at her. "Do not doubt me, Sir. I know my way."

"The night is dark. Are you sure you know your way?"

Joan tells him, "I am like an owl. I can see. I would not be here if I got lost easily, Sir." Major Johnson gives her a pass and his ring. He tells her, "The Captain will know who you are and that you are with me when you show him this ring."

She takes the ring and tells him, "Very well."

He walks to his door and instructs Jacob, his aide, "Get her the fasted horse we have and make sure she has something to eat."

"Yes, Sir, " Jacob responds to his request. The Major tells her, "I will send one of my men to help you through the pickets. I will pray for you after that."

Before she leaves, she asks him, "What did you find out about the soldier I was telling you about?"

He looks at her and tells her, "You were so right!"

CHAPTER THIRTY-TWO

BALLROOM DANCE

Joan takes a deep breath and squares her shoulders as she prepares for the hardest battle of her life - keeping up the pretense of detesting the very soldiers she must respect and esteem. While sitting around the campfire, she watches the men eat ravenously the stew and cornbread. She watches as everyone gets ready for the battle of their life. As she comes near Major Johnson, he lifts his eyes toward her. He is proud of the scouting job she does for him. He has never met anyone like her. She is full of decency and dignity and will sacrifice her life for her country. He can see why President Davis gave her to him as his scout. She is good and fast, and she does her job well.

As she sits watching everyone, a chorus of chuckles arises from the men. As Joan looks around at each one of the soldier's faces by the fire, she knows each of them accepts hardships that are certainly more painful than wounds or physical suffering. They do not receive any glory or even acknowledgment for their sacrifices as she has done.

Joan clears her throat and informs them, "I am going to take a nap. We have to be up at 3:00 for battle." As Joan stands up, she tilts her head and looks around, wondering how many of these men will make it through. She tries to do every one of them a great service as a scout. Even though they are still not at war, she will still defend her troops because there are still men out there with hate and want to fight.

At 2:45, the Major gives the order, "To mount." Within minutes, Joan and the major's men are in their saddles, heading down the road to their next obligation.

The war is at the end, and it is time for everyone to have some fun. The men of the war have been fighting for four years and sleeping on the ground. As they ride, it is a quiet morning with no one wanting to fight. Joan can't believe she is going home for a while and is going dancing.

When she gets home, Dora is so excited to see her. She grabs her as she comes in the door, mud and all. Dora doesn't care because her friend is home. Together the girls go up the stairs, arm, and arms to talk. Jim and Jane had picked up Joan at the camp and let Joan and Dora have some time together.

Joan falls on Dora's bed, and they are hysterically laughing. Joan tells Dora, "We are going to have a dance at the base, and I need a dress." Dora and Joan retrieve the perfect fabric. Joan tells Dora, I want you to come with me to the dance."

Dora comments, "She and Paul are engaged, and she doesn't think it is a proper thing to do."

Joan works all night on her dress for the dance. She is tired of wearing a uniform and wants the men to see what she looks like in a beautiful ballroom gown. Most ladies will change their clothes sometimes around six times a day. Joan is aware that they have an outfit for breakfast, church, tweeds for after church, a tea dress, an afternoon dress, a visiting dress, a dinner dress, and finally, your nightclothes. You can't wear the same dinner dress twice in one week, and that's not even getting into special occasions like going riding or to a party. Joan doesn't have time for all of this. She was a soldier.

It takes all night, but Joan finishes her dress. It is white down the front with pink lace down both sides. Little bows are at the top of her shoulders, and a big bow is on the back of her waist. Joan and Dora are the same sizes. She borrows one of Dora's corsets for her waist.

The dominant aesthetic of the mid-nineteenth century calls for full skirts, and ladies wear corsets before the common wearing of the crinoline. Also, several petticoats provide this fullness. Joan uses a corset to constrict her waist and create slenderness. Every woman wears a corset. Some of the slender young debutantes affect the dramatic princess look. To look stylish, thousands of women wear dresses with the waist so tight that isn't any free movement of the upper body. Some ladies put their bonnets on before attempting the painful ordeal of getting into glove-fitting dress waists.

Three hours before the dance, Joan has Dora help her get into her dress. Dora helps her with the tight lacing and then helps her put her dress over everything. Dora does Joan's hair up and in a bun at the back of her neck. Dora helps her get her shoes on right before she walks down the stairs.

Joan makes sure her dress has short sleeves with a full skirt that doesn't drag on the floor. Joan's hair is black, so she wears white and pink. The pink compliments her hair. Joan's ball gown is the most delicately and exotically timed with luxurious fabrics. Her gown is the most formal attire for the dance. She trims the silk with lace, pearls, sequins, ribbons, and ruffles. The layer upon layer of petticoats gives her dress the desired fullness. It is not too hot or heavy to wear.

As Joan lifts the front of her dress to come down the stairs, Jim, Jane, and Dora are waiting for her at the bottom. She is so pretty and graceful coming down. Jim bends his arm to escort her to the carriage for the night.

Major Johnson's hospitality at balls is famous, and his love of festivity is renowned among the female residents of the region. As Joan comes into the ballroom, the men notice how beautiful she is. They are not aware that this is Ace. Joan watches the men whirling their partners around the room with enthusiasm as she walks over to a seat. As Joan enters, Major Johnson takes a second look at her. He can't believe that this beautiful girl is Ace from the battlefield with a beautiful gown, makeup on, and hair on top of her head. His heart does a flip-flop in his chest. The men can't wait to stop dancing to go over to her to put their names on her dance card. Joan will look at her dance card and let them know if it is full or not. She is having the time of her life. This is what she needs… to have some fun.

Major Johnson is enjoying himself. He enjoys the company of women and is as comfortable in a ballroom as on a horse's back. Making his way across the room, he asks Joan, "To dance." He innocently flirts with her as they dance. He can't take his eyes off her. As they are dancing, Major Williams nods toward the open door of the balcony. The Major walks Joan back to her chair after the dance as he removes his hand from hers and asks her for another dance later.

Joan looks at her card and tells him, "We have the fourth dance."

When the two men stood alone outside, a soldier gives the Major the message he locates in the oak tree. "Some men are burning homes, and the enemy is near." He tells the Major.

As he reads the message, he tells Williams, "Very good." Joan has left him a note, and when he looks at her, she knows he has her message that some men from the Union are getting close to the dance. The Major begins to see how important Ace is to him, just as long as she has his back.

The Major asks Joan if she wants to walk outside with him as he takes her hand. As they walk outside by the railing, he notices that the horses are causing a raucous on the picket line. He asks Joan, "When did you find out about them coming?"

Joan tells him, "About an hour ago."

As he looks into her eyes, he tells her, "To stay here. I will see what my men are doing. I don't want you to get mud all over your beautiful dress."

He goes outside and tells one of the soldiers what to do,' and the soldier hurries to follow his order.

Major Johnson is standing on the porch, thinking about what to do. A light touch on his arm interrupts him. "Major Johnson?" Major Johnson turns around to see a lady standing there. "Yes, ma'am," as he looks at her, he assumes she is around nineteen.

He asks her, "What may I do for you, young lady?"

"I am Susan Goddard. I want to talk to you about one of your men who asked me to marry him."

"Oh, I see. And who is the lucky man?"

"Andy Williams, Sir." Major Johnson looks deeply into her eyes and then smiles knowingly.

"He is a good man. One of my best officers. You are very lucky to have him as your husband."

Joan is dancing with another soldier. Susan takes a step closer to the Major. "I pity her especially tonight," looking at Joan. "Especially with all those angry men."

The Major steps back and looks at her, "What, men?"

Susan takes a step back and doesn't want to tell him. "The Alton brothers," she said in a whisper. "They are waiting for her when she leaves here tonight."

Major Johnson tells her, "Excuse me," and he walks over to Joan.

"I am taking you home right now. Let's go!"

As Major Johnson escorts Joan to the wagon, he instructs his men to follow him. He helps Joan up on the seat and hits the horses' reins again the horses.

He tells them, "Let's go."

As they ride, Joan looks at him and asks him, "May I ask what is going on?"

He looks at her and tells her, "The Alton brothers are waiting for you on your way home." The Major helps Joan out of the wagon and tells her, "To stay inside the rest of the night. That is an order, Ace!" Joan isn't happy about it, but she obeys him.

The Alton brothers are always causing trouble, and he doesn't want Joan hurt. As he turns the wagon around, he tells his men, "Let's visit the Alton brothers." As they pull up in front of the Alton brothers' home, Jake comes out of the front door.

Can I help you, Major?" he says.

"You sure can, Jake. I am aware that you and your brothers are waiting for my officer tonight as she heads home. If I hear of this again, I will be back with my troops and take you in, and you won't like it. Do I make myself clear!"

Jake tells him, "Yes, sir."

Jake scurries inside and tells his brothers, "I guess we better find someone else to bother. Major Johnson will hang us up over her! He laughs as he lies down on his bed.

Major Johnson rides back to Joan's home and knocks on the door. He is surprised she was still there. Joan comes to the door, and Major Johnson asks her to come outside on the porch. He informs her, "I talked to the Alton brothers, and they will not bother you tonight."

Major looks at Joan as she stands there still in her beautiful gown. His heart does another flip-flop in his chest as he looks at her face. He slowly takes her in his arms and gives her a lovely kiss. He falls in love with Joan and tells her, "You are the most beautiful women I have ever met."

Joan swallows hard and looks at him for a few moments. This gives him time to study her face. She looks back at him as she pauses to digest what he has just said. It was a strong face, handsome, and could tell he that he spoke to her from his heart.

After a few long moments, she tilts her head back, exposing white flesh above her collar and looks at him with serious intent, and lets him kiss her again. Johnson takes a step closer. He looks back at her as he walks down the steps to his wagon. He smiles and tells her, "I will see you in the morning, Ace," and rides down the road.

Major Johnson walks in his front door and walks over to the fire as he throws up his hands and begins to pace. He knows he doesn't need it, but he is falling in love with Joan. She is a good scout, and she informs him that one of his men is a spy. He walks over to his desk and sits on his desk with his arms crossed. He examines the note she delivers to him before the dance. In the wagon, on her way, home Joan informs him that a man has been reporting his numbers, his movements, and his plans to the Union.

He asks her, "How?"

She tells him, "You technically have three companies, but they number less than two. Your recent supplies include a cannon and two dozen tanks." As they ride, he wonders how could one of his men betrays him. She tells him, "You are the authority in the south, and they don't like it. This is why they want to stop you."

Johnson explains to her, "War is never simple." He stares back at her. ."What do you suggest I do about it?"

Joan looks at him and says, "What will you do with any prisoner with whom you had suspicion?"

He laughs and gazes at her with a skeptical look, " I will imprison such a person and question him as long as the day is long."

Joan smiles up at him and tells him, "Then you have your answer."

Major Johnson sighs and leans his hands for a moment on the mantle over the fireplace as he considers his next move. He is only twenty-five, but he feels old. In the past, he lived the life of a gentleman in a setting of refinement and repose. Now, he is the Major of a large band of men, and he has to make life-and-death decisions on behalf of his country. He wants out but knows it was important to be here.

Johnson is aware that Joan is somewhat childlike and feminine at the age of eighteen. In contrast, there is a solid aspect of hardened steel about her. She has been a slave for seven years to Master Jenkins. He can tell her mind is not idle, nor is it fretful, even when she is staring straight ahead. She tells him, "No trials can be more difficult than those I experience as a slave." She looks out the window again as if she is going to stay on the subject for him. He tells her, "I don't want to send you out by yourself. I can't help but wonder if it isn't worth the risk and cost?"

Joan doesn't' turn around as she tells him, "I will die for my country. If you find the traitor, it will be worth the cost, Major." Joan speaks with calm assurance as she looks out the window.

Johnson knows she has energy, conviction, and sincerity in her manner. These attributes somewhat silence his reservations and mistrust of a woman. Although, he worries about her ability to endure a night in captivity if they capture her. As she turns around and looks at him, her countenance reflects cool courage and commitment. Her deep brown eyes speak of defiance, strong will, and strength, enlightening him that it will take more than a night of fighting to diminish her determination. He knows she will play the game to the end. War is no game to her; liberty for her country is enough of a payment for her. Johnson walks over and takes Joan in his arms. Her acceptance of her fate radiates in her eyes, but her face is destitute of all other expressions. He doesn't want to let go of her. Never is anything so frail, and yet, with determination and resolute as she is. As he kisses her and lets go of her. She looks into his eyes as she walks out the door.

As the Major stands in the middle of the room, he fights to himself as her eyes strike him at the most noticcable feature of all. They are not of a stunning hue, not a light brown or dark. Instead, they reflect a deep blending of the two. They are both intense and overpowering. They reveal nothing as far as emotion; yet, he can see she cares for him as he does for her. Her natural dark complexion deepens with exposure to the sun and wind, making her appear quite beautiful.

As the Major is thinking of Joan, a loud knock is on his door. The latch clicks open, and an officer stands, breathing heavily on the threshold. Johnson looks at the officer as he looks around from the window. Major Johnson looks at the officer again and says, "Yes?"

The officer was out of breath as he tells Major Johnson, "The Union is upon us, and they are shooting at officer Shell."

Major Johnson runs out of the door as he instructs the officer, "Get my men and let's go." Joan is riding back toward the gates as fast as Lighting can go. The Union is coming closer to her as she leans to the side as she rode. Major Johnson's men start shooting at the Union and cover Joan as she rides through the gate.

As Joan gets off her horse, Major Johnson tells her, " That is it! Get in my office now! That is an order, officer Shell!" As Joan enters his office, she shuts the door! Major Johnson is pacing the floor. He looks up at her and tells her, "That is it, Joan; I love you, and I can't have you out there with bullets buzzing by you or one hitting you. Do you understand this, Joan?"

Joan looks at him and says, "Yes, Sir." Major Johnson walks around to his chair and falls into it as his hands are going in his hair.

" I am sending you to the hospital to be a nurse. No more scouting for you! "

Joan opens her mouth and tells him, "But Major Johnson, I love what I do."

He tells her, "I don't care!" He gets up and walks around in front of her as he asks her, "Will you marry me?"

Joan looks at him and teases him, "Is that an order, Major Johnson?" She smiles up at him.

He looks at her and tells her, "If that is what it takes!"

Joan has experience working as a nurse on the battlefield with men being shot and their legs shot off. She has been there praying for them as they take their last breaths. Joan works in the army hospital where soldiers are recovering from disease or injury. Joan is helping the sicker soldiers with injuries. As Joan walks through the ward, men lie on rotten straw; nurses are suffering and need to be in bed themselves. But, these nurses keep going because there are so many hurt men.

In 1861 things begin to change with the creation of the U.S. Sanitary Commission. This private organization is recognized by the federal government and run by civilians. Its mission is to generate financial support to meet the medical needs of the military from the battlefields, acquire and distribute food, clothing, and medical supplies to soldiers and military hospitals, organize military hospitals and camps and arrange transportation for the wounded.

Joan is going from field hospitals and even onto the battlefield after the firing stops. A lot of the hotels are turned into hospitals where she helps soldiers with injuries. Joan only has training on the battlefield. She does not have any of the activities required to work as a nurse. Joan has a copy of the

1837 handbook, The Family Nurse, and refers to it when she needs it; otherwise, she learns on the job. Her duties vary depending on whether she serves in hospitals, field hospitals close to the battlefields, or on the battlefields themselves after the fighting stops. Every day is different. She doesn't know from day to day if she will be assisting surgeons, changing dressings, washing patients, preparing meals, feeding men, emptying bedpans and chamber pots, or administering medications. She also writes letters to the men's families at home. She doesn't get much sleep; maybe, if she is lucky, three hours a day.

Joan works long hours in extremely difficult conditions. She is driven by compassion, putting her own life at risk, and often suffering the outright contempt of surgeons and military officials. Joan tells Major Johnson, "One night after two years, I realize that being a nurse is as important as being a spy. "

Dora and Joan are talking one night, "About how many women can't make a living with their men off to war."

Joan tells him, " A lot of women follow the troops and make themselves useful where they can safely earn money, have food, and lodging. During this time, many nurses are being recognized and starting training programs, and I am thinking about joining them. When women are doing the nursing, this means there is one more man to do the fighting. Joan informs Dora, " I will be getting two dollars a month, and I can supervise the nurses and act as go-betweens to the surgeons and receive four dollars a month."

Joan heads back to the ward, but it is nice to visit with Dora for an hour. As Joan walks through the long ward, it is difficult for her to return to the gaze of the occupants in the forty-two beds. She walks along, helping each soldier, and with a sinking heart, she raises the head of a poor fellow in the last stages of yellow fever to give him a soothing drink of water.

During the two years at the hospital, Joan writes long letters to Dora and records her daily experience in diaries at the end of her shift. On most days, the routine begins at 5:00 with the sound of reveille and ends at 9:00 p.m. when the night nurse takes over. After dinner at noon, sometimes if the soldiers don't need her, she will rest or walk around the hospital looking at birds by the river. Much of her remaining time is full of non-medical tasks, writing letters for the men, and attending to the many hospital visitors. Sometimes she will spend the evening with patients singing and playing cards or music.

As Joan sits at her table one evening, adding to the list of medicines, writing down the name, regiment, list of clothing, etc., of the new arrivals, and separating her from her other world, someone puts his hands over her eyes. This surprises Joan, and she doesn't know who it is. Major Johnson sees her as if it has been two weeks since he last looks into her eyes. Joan is excited as he put his arms around her and tells her, "I am kidnapping you for the day."

Joan informs him, "I can't just walk off the floor and leave."

He tells her, "Yes, you can, and that is an order!" As he smiles at her. "I have a nurse covering for you."

Major Andy Johnson makes a picnic for them, and he wants to ride down by the lake with her this afternoon.

Andy is aware that the picnic food should be simple, light, and fun, just like a summer day. He finds an old-school picnic basket at his friend's home, places a container of coffee, flatware for the pie, some cloth napkins, two cups for the coffee, a large blanket, bug spray, and sunscreen, with fried chicken, potato salad, tart, and baked beans and places the basket in the back of the wagon. He helps Joan up on the seat, kisses her, picks up the reins, and starts toward the lake.

The weather is beautiful. The sun is shining as Andy pulls the wagon up by the lake. There is a tree for shade. Andy is laughing as he helps Joan down, and together they walk hand and hand to the tree. Andy sets the basket down and takes Joan in his arms. Joan passionately looks up at him as they lay down on the blanket. Rarely has a woman ever made his heart feel like this, yet he knows he is in love with her. She has unusual dignity and self-assurance, and there is a strange fire in her eyes. Joan is the most important person in his life and will be until one of them dies.

A romantic picnic is just the thing for them to help them celebrate their love for each other. It is fun, and casual and allows them to spend quality time together. Andy and Joan sit down and look out over the lake; it is a beautiful place to relax and enjoy each other's company with minimal distractions. As they pull out the food and lay it on the blanket, Joan looks up and sees a botanical garden with beautiful blooms. Andy walks over and picks her some flowers to go with the meal. Andy creates a romantic picnic with a perfect atmosphere; the beautiful flowers add to the intimate picnic.

As Andy and Joan lay on the blanket after eating. Andy tells her, "No picnic is complete without a book for both of us and finger food. "Andy has nuts, gourmet cheese, with a heart-shaped dessert, easy snacks to go with the bottle of wine, and two wine glasses. Andy uses cookie cutters from the kitchen to create a watermelon heart shape.

Even though Andy brings two books to read, they discover that reading together and to each other can be a highly romantic activity between a kiss or two. They have a great day, but it is time to go as the sun sets in the west. Andy helps Joan up, and together they walk hand and hand to the wagon. Andy kisses Joan one more time before helping her up into the seat. It couldn't have been a better day for both of them.

Made in the USA
Columbia, SC
26 August 2023

22065750R00141